THE LAST FLEET

ERIC S BROWN

SEVERED PRESS
HOBART TASMANIA

THE LAST FLEET

ISBN: 978-1-925493-95-5

THE LAST FLEET

The *Laybourne* shook as another missile slammed into her portside. Ashely cursed as the impact caused her to lose her balance. She landed hard on the docking bay floor. Before she could even try to get up herself, Eliot grabbed her, yanking her to her feet.

"Come on!" he shouted, dragging her with him towards the half-loaded transport that was powering up not more than twenty yards from their position.

Ashley wasn't an engineer, but she could tell that the missile had broken the *Laybourne*'s back. The battleship was damaged beyond repair. She'd never blink again. That meant, with no hope of running, the *Laybourne* was dead. It was only a question of how long she could hold on.

There was no time to finish loading up the remainder of the gear, parts, and supplies that sat near the transport. It was time to go, or the transport would die along with the *Laybourne*.

Wiggins stood in the side door of the transport waving them on as the two of them ran across the docking bay. Eliot shoved her in first and quickly followed after her. With a heave, Wiggins slammed the door closed, signaling for the pilot to take off.

The transport lurched as it lifted from the floor of the bay and angled itself to face the opening hanger doors that led out into space. Ashley looked around the interior of the transport and frowned at just how few other marines there were aboard it. There had been two transports prepping to flee the *Laybourne* in case things went south. She hoped both of them were going to make it. Of course, even getting off the battleship before it was blown apart didn't guarantee survival. They had to get well clear of the *Laybourne* in order to be able to blink away, and they'd be under heavy fire most likely until they were able to do so.

"Punch it!" she heard Wiggins shout as she strapped herself in for the ride.

The transport shot forward like a bullet from the barrel of a gun. It roared through the hangar doors out into the midst of the battle surrounding the *Laybourne*. Ashley held on tight as the transport broke hard to starboard, its engines straining as its pilot pushed them to their max.

The next minute and a half was much the same as the transport flew towards the *Pickman*. Ashley hated the fear and helplessness that clawed at her, but there was nothing she could do but continue to hold on and pray. Whether she lived or died was up to how good the pilot was and random luck. She hadn't had time to don her helmet. Without it, she couldn't even listen on the communications chatter to try to overhear what was happening.

"We're going in hot!" Eliot yelled at her, motioning for her to hold on tight as if she wasn't already.

The bottom of the transport slammed down onto what must have been the docking bay floor of the *Pickman*. Even through the armored hull, she could hear the screeching of metal as the transport skidded to a halt. As it finally stopped moving, Ashley vomited the contents of her stomach all over the front of her combat suit and the straps of the harness that secured her in place. She didn't care though. Eliot shot her a thumbs up and Ashley knew they had made it aboard the *Pickman*.

****

Captain Harrison watched the *Laybourne* blow apart as a Swarm destroyer emptied its missile tubes into it at near point-blank range. He supposed he should be used to this kind of carnage by now but doubted that he ever would be. He felt the tips of his fingernails pierce the flesh of his palm inside his clenched right fist and the warm trickle of blood that flowed over the side of his hand to drip onto the arm of his command chair. Harrison released his fist and shook his hand at the unexpected pain.

The *Pickman*'s shields shimmered as she took another series of direct hits from one of the Swarm battleships she was engaged with. Her shields held, if barely.

"More power to the forward shields!" his XO, Allen, yelled.

"What's the status of the transports from the *Laybourne*?" Captain Harrison demanded.

"Sir!" Allen snapped back at him. "The transports from the *Laybourne* are onboard!"

"Then what are we waiting for?" Captain Harrison growled.

"Admiral Powell hasn't ordered the fleet to disengage yet, sir," Allen told him.

Captain Harrison kept his thoughts about the admiral to himself as he leaned forward in his seat. "I don't care. The *Laybourne* and the *Nicholson* are gone. Start blink prep and get us the hell out of here."

Allen went pale at the rage in his voice but followed his orders. "All hands, prepare for blink!" Allen shouted over the ship-wide comm. as the *Pickman*'s astrogation tech, Reynolds, doubled over his station making the necessary calculations to blink them to the pre-agreed upon rendezvous coordinates.

"We're being hailed, sir!" Claudia, the comm. officer, informed him. "It's Admiral Powell."

"Put it through." Captain Harrison nodded at her.

The *Pickman*'s weapon crews were returning fire at the two Swarm battleships. The ship's forward railguns hammered at the shields of the portside Swarm battleship while a volley of missiles left her tubes bound for the one more to her starboard side. The first ship's shields held against the barrage of railgun fire, though it did bank sideways in space in a failed attempt at an evasive maneuver. Countermeasures sprayed from the second Swarm battleship, cutting the number of missiles heading towards it in half. Its point defense systems took out a good number more, but even so, some of the *Pickman*'s missiles made it through. The second Swarm battleship's shields were inoperable, so the missiles that did strike the armor of its hull blew gaping holes that leaked atmosphere in its forward sections. Captain Harrison allowed himself a smile at the sight of the damaged Swarm ship as it poured on speed and overshot the *Pickman* attempting to get out of range of her forward weapons.

"Captain Harrison!" Admiral Powell's voice rang out across the *Pickman*'s bridge as Claudia patched him through.

Captain Harrison ignored the admiral long enough to shout, "Take that bastard with our aft tubes!"

"Firing!" the chief weapons officer, Bloch, ordered from his station on the other side of the bridge.

A trio of high-velocity torpedoes left the *Pickman*'s aft tubes and burnt their way through the void towards the fleeing Swarm battleship. They smashed into it, one after another, each creating a blast of heat and light that melted armor and ripped holes in the fleeing battleship's hull. The already-damaged Swarm battleship lurched as its main engines looked to go offline.

"Harrison!" Powell screamed again.

"Admiral," Captain Harrison answered finally, "I'm afraid I am a bit busy at the moment, sir."

The tide of the battle around the *Pickman* continued to shift in favor of the Swarm fleet. Captain Harrison knew that they had never really stood a chance of taking the Demond system from the bugs, no matter what Admiral Powell had believed. The number of Swarm ships in the system had tripled since their arrival with more blinking in even now. Demond was just too close to Swarm space to be a realistic target, no matter how small its initial defense fleet had been. Like always, the bugs had swept in, kicked the crap of them, and were presently forcing them into yet another retreat.

"Sir," Claudia reported, "Admiral Powell has ended the closed transmission I patched through."

Captain Harrison grunted his acknowledgement. For all his faults, the admiral wasn't a complete fool. By now, even Powell could see that the fleet's only hope of survival was to once again abandon its target and run.

"The admiral has given fleet-wide orders to disengage and withdraw, sir," Claudia added.

"Then what are we waiting for? Mr. Boyes, blink us out of here!" Captain Harrison ordered.

"Yes, sir!" Boyes, the helmsman, snapped as he activated the ship's blink drive. The *Pickman* vanished in a flash of light as several volleys of missiles came tearing through the space it had just occupied.

****

Ashley stumbled from the transport, thankful to be alive. One of the *Pickman*'s hangar crew close by reached to help her. She gave him a look that sent the man retreating from her sight. She was a marine after all and had an image to keep up. In all, the once great Marine Corps of the Republic now numbered less than twenty thousand. They were spread out across the various ships of the fleet Admiral Powell commanded, with the bulk of them stationed aboard the fleet's two remaining carrier ships. In its prime, the Corps had consisted of millions of the best troopers the known galaxies had ever known. So many had died in the last two years, and not just those of the Marine Corps.

When the first Swarm ship had entered Republic space, no one, not even the Navy, had seen the aliens as much of a threat. That ship had attacked Octvey II, one of the Republic's most outlying colonies, and paid the price for it. The system's patrolling cruisers were more than a match for it. That ship had time though to send a message to the rest of the Swarm. Less than a week later, both colonies in the Octvey system were destroyed, and the Republic had found itself at war with an enemy straight out of the depths of Hell.

Battles raged all across the Republic's frontier as the Navy scrambled every available ship it had to intercept the massive armada of Swarm ships that suddenly flooded the Octvey system and began to push their way inward, deeper into the Republic's territory. The rest was history. The Republic fell, its core worlds overrun and taken by the Swarm. The scattered remnants of its Navy regrouped into the last fleet humankind would likely ever crew. That fleet, under Admiral Powell's command, had taken the name Taskforce Hope. An ironic name because even a grunt like she knew there was no hope left at all.

Ashley jumped as she was torn from her thoughts by the sound of Elliot's booming voice behind her.

"That was one heck of a ride!" he almost shouted, sauntering up beside her.

"Says you," she grunted at him.

Ignoring her comment, Elliot beamed at her. "Let's report in and get some chow. I'm starving."

The shuffling around of marine personnel was a common occurrence in Taskforce Hope. Reporting in and finding out what unit they would be attached to, hadn't taken long at all. Their new direct C.O. was a lieutenant named Clarkson.

The *Pickman* was a sharp contrast to the *Laybourne*. The *Laybourne* had been an older ship even at the start of the Swarm War. The *Pickman* though was one of the final battleships to roll off the line before the fleet yards around Earth itself had been destroyed.

"Stop staring at the walls." Elliot elbowed her as they walked down the corridor towards the ship's mess hall. "You're creeping me out."

"Hold up!" a voice called out to them. A young marine, who had to be a recent draft from Taskforce Hope's small civilian population, came running up to them.

"You're from the *Laybourne* right?" he asked and then continued without waiting for either of them to answer, "I'm Gary, Gary Weston, part of Lieutenant Clarkson's platoon."

"Good to meet you, kid." Elliot nodded at the young man. "You can call me Elliot and this here is Ashley."

Ashley hated getting to know people. It seemed a pointless thing to do when they could be dead in a matter of hours if the Swarm attacked. Taskforce Hope was always on the run. Not so much fleeing the Swarm as rather hiding from it and biding its time until the brass figured out where it was best to hit the Swarm next.

The three of them entered the mess hall together. There were very few people there. Most of the *Pickman*'s personnel had to be dealing with the damage from the battle they had just escaped from or unloading and cataloging the meager amount of supplies, parts, and ordinance that the surviving transports from the *Laybourne* had brought onboard.

Though the *Pickman* itself was impressive, the food in her mess hall was pretty standard fare. Ashley took a plate of potatoes, covered in weak-looking gravy that made her lips curl up at the sight of it, half a roll, and a slab of something that was supposed to be pork to a table at the rear of the mess. The potatoes looked to be real but the rest, without question, came from the ship's store of MREs.

Food was food to Elliot though. He started shoveling the contents of his plate into his mouth as soon as his butt hit his seat.

The newbie marine, Weston, sat with them, watching them with wide-eyed fascination.

"Are you guys seen a lot of action?" Weston asked.

Ashley winced at the question. Just how new was this kid?

Elliot laughed through a mouthful of potatoes though. "Kid, do you know who you're sitting with? Ashley here is the hero of the Delta Niner."

"You're that Ashley?" Weston nearly dropped his fork.

"Let it be," Ashley told him.

"She doesn't like to talk about it much," Elliot said, "but yeah, she's that Ashley."

Weston sat up straighter over his plate. "Ma'am, it's an honor to meet you."

"I said, let it be." Ashley's tone was that of a warning.

Weston shut his mouth, but he continued to stare at her.

"So, this Lieutenant Clarkson," Elliot spoke up. "I've never heard of him. Is he a newbie too?"

"Yes, sir," Weston answered. "He was just promoted a month ago. The Helldogs are his first command."

"Heh." Ashley smirked. "The Helldogs, I like the sound of that."

Weston was nodding rapidly. "We're a new drop unit that Captain Harrison only ordered be put together recently."

Ashley didn't bother to try to conceal her sigh as Elliot winked at her.

"You hear that, Ashley," he said as he finished his potatoes and started in on his pork with a vengeance. "Looks like we're going to be babysitting again."

****

Admiral Jerimiah Powell paced the spacious bridge of the super dreadnaught, the *Homestead*, trying to control his anger. The Swarm had driven Taskforce Hope away from its target in utter defeat once again. The Demond system should have been a victory for the taskforce. All the intel pointed to it being a system they should have been able to take and hold, at least long enough to acquire much-needed supplies. To make matters worse, many of his captains were pushing the limits of open mutiny against his overall command of the taskforce. Captain Harrison might not be chief among them, but he angered Powell the most. Harrison's motives weren't simply the usual greed for more power or the desire to fight the war his way against the Swarm. No, Harrison was driven by a sincere belief that Taskforce Hope needed to live up to its name. The man wanted to abandon the war and flee into the uncharted regions of the universe to start over. That was what made him dangerous, his mixed up principles. Even though Captain Harrison, for the most part, kept his views to himself, there was a growing number who had begun to share them. Something needed to be done about Harrison, and soon, but for now, Powell had other matters to attend to.

"I want full, active scans of this entire system," Powell ordered. "All ships are to remain at alert status. Repairs on any battle damage taken are to begin at once. Do I make myself clear?"

Captain Smith nodded and headed off to make sure his orders were carried out. The *Homestead* was Taskforce Hope's flagship. Admiral Powell watched the little man go. Smith was far from one of the best captains in Taskforce Hope. He was too much of a "by the book" leader to think outside of the box, even when it was the only way to survive. However, his loyalty was unshakeable, and Powell knew he could trust Captain Smith with his life.

The *Homestead* was Taskforce Hope's sole remaining super dreadnought. The massive ship was ten times larger than a Republic battleship. Its shields and heavy armor made it pretty much a mobile fortress in space. Oh, it had teeth too, packing enough firepower to almost lay waste to an entire planet on its own, but Powell had chosen it as his flagship mainly because it had already been the heart of the Taskforce when his original flagship, the *Wolf*, had been lost. The giant super dreadnought's crew numbered in the thousands, and it carried several hundred of the few surviving civilians of the Republic as well. The *Homestead*, despite her armor and advanced weapons systems, wasn't entirely a ship of the line anymore. She also served as one of Taskforce Hope's primary manufacturing ships. A good portion of her mass had been given up to growing food, producing armaments and medical supplies, etc. Most of the fleet's limited civilian population was carried aboard her as well.

There was no government anymore. The entire, last fleet of the Republic lived under martial law. Powell's word was law, and he had recognized that fact as the opportunity it was. Under his leadership, Taskforce Hope had been able to carry on the war against the Swarm and even now, with its resources depleted, there was a chance of victory over the bugs that had driven the human race from their homes. Powell swore he would make the Swarm pay, whatever the cost.

"Admiral," Robinson, the *Homestead*'s XO, approached him. "As usual, this ship escaped taking any serious damage, sir, but there are several ships in the taskforce who are reporting that their repairs may take the better part of a week or more."

"Dispatch what personnel we can spare to assist them, but inform those captains that they have two days at most to complete whatever repairs their ships need. If we remain in this system any longer than that, we may find ourselves engaged by the Swarm and on their terms this time," Powell said. "The sooner we're able to get underway again, the better."

Robinson acknowledged his orders but continued to linger near his command chair.

"What is it, Robinson?" Powell demanded.

"How long has it been since you last slept, sir?" Robinson asked cautiously.

Powell started to snap at the XO until he realized he couldn't remember.

Taking Powell's silence as license to continue, Robinson said, "May I suggest you take some time now, sir? So far, the scans being conducted haven't revealed any sign of Swarm ships in this system. If they do show up while we're here, we'll need you at your best, sir."

Powell's lips twitched into a twisted, mockery of a smile at Robinson's well-chosen words.

"I suppose I can't argue that, Mr. Robinson," Powell said, getting up from his command chair. "I'll be in my quarters."

Robinson bowed slightly to him and said, "I shall contact you at once should any kind of situation arise, sir."

Powell left the bridge. Instead of heading directly for his quarters, however, he paid a visit to Dr. Spinner. Spinner was the head of the fleet's severely limited and overworked science division. Not long after Taskforce Hope had assembled in the wake of the Republic's destruction and began its war against the Swarm, Powell had tasked Spinner with finding a means for Taskforce Hope to make the Swarm pay. Spinner was a leading xenobiologist. Powell had faith that if anyone could produce a bio-weapon capable of inflicting extreme if not genocidal losses on the Swarm, it was Spinner. Spinner had protested at first, not wanting any part of Powell's quest for vengeance on the bugs. His efforts had been halfhearted. However, after Spinner's wife, one of the fleet's medical doctors, had been lost aboard the Duran, Spinner had finally come around. Since that time, Spinner devoted his every waking moment with an almost religious zeal to creating the weapon Powell demanded of him. Even so, Powell was still waiting on the weapon he dreamed of that could wipe the Swarm out of existence once and for all.

Spinner had been given five labs and almost unlimited access to anything that the doctor needed from both the *Homestead* and all the other ships of Taskforce Hope. One of those five labs had become Spinner's personal workspace. Its lights were dim as Admiral Powell entered. Two large holding cells filled the center of the lab. Inside one of them was the corpse of a Swarm Queen. The female bug's bloated body lay on the floor of her cell. She had been alive the last time Powell had visited Spinner and her death brought the admiral hope that Dr. Spinner had finally made some sort of a breakthrough.

The other cell contained a typical warrior of the Swarm. The head of the bipedal bug very much resembled that of an Earth ant. Twin, vicious mandibles clicked together over its mouth at the sight of him. The bottom sides of the bug's human-shaped arms were lined with razor sharp ridges between its three-fingered hands and its ball-shaped elbows. The warrior threw itself at Powell, crashing into the thick, reinforced glass of its cell with a loud thud. Neither the glass nor the creature's exoskeleton cracked, but sparks flew as the warrior tried to cut its way through the glass with the blades on the undersides of its arms to get at him.

Spinner's squeaky voice rang out from the rear of the lab. "Admiral Powell, what have I told you about riling up my specimens?"

Powell laughed and pointed at the corpse in the other cell. "The queen is dead. Should I get my hopes up that you're onto something?"

"I might be," Spinner sighed. "It's too early to say for sure though."

Powell gave the unkempt scientist a stern look.

"We're running tests now to discover if the virus that killed her is viable as a weapon."

"It killed her, did it not?" Powell argued.

"Yes, as far as we can tell, it was our virus that killed her and not merely her prolonged incarceration here." Spinner nodded. "That said, there are many variables that need to be worked out before we can be sure it will affect all queens of the Swarm in such a manner, not to mention within the atmospheres of bug ships."

"I see," Powell said, though he really didn't fully understand what Spinner meant. Like the bug that still lived, he was a warrior and not a scientist. "How long then until you have something for me?"

"It's hard to say," Spinner shrugged. "There's much work yet to be done."

"Best case?" Powell pressed.

"A few weeks," Spinner frowned, "and that's if everything checks out perfectly."

Powell tried to hide his excitement. It was the best estimate Spinner had ever given him during the man's near two-year work on the project.

"A few weeks." Powell smiled despite himself as he repeated the words.

"That's best case," Spinner reminded him stubbornly.

They had worked out a delivery method for such a virus during Spinner's first year on the project. Finding a virus that worked had been all that was holding them back. Now, that virus appeared to be on the edge of completion.

"I'll leave you to it then, Doctor," Powell said and turned to leave. "But keep me posted on your progress."

"As always, Admiral." Powell nodded.

Powell left the lab feeling absolutely giddy. Whistling a tune, he strolled along the corridor heading for his personal quarters to get some much-needed rest. Before he hit his bed, he paused long enough to send orders to Colonel Chero, the head of the taskforce's internal security forces. Captain Harrison had to be dealt with. Taskforce Hope was on the verge of victory against the Swarm and nothing could be allowed to endanger it. Too many lives had been lost to allow all those men, women, and children to have died in vain.

****

Harrison sat at his desk in his ready room staring at the data on Taskforce Hope's engagement with the Swarm in the Demond system. Frustrated at not seeing anything new about the Swarm's tactics in how they had dealt with the taskforce's latest intrusion into Swarm space, he called up the *Pickman*'s inventory lists instead. They told a grim tale of just how desperate things were for Taskforce Hope in general. Harrison knew the *Pickman* was one of the taskforce's best supplied and equipped ships, short of the *Homestead*, and that worried him a great deal. The *Pickman*'s stores contained roughly three weeks of food without putting his crew back on limited rations again. Over a month had passed since there had been any chance for the taskforce to pick up supplies from an unpopulated planet. It had been even longer since it had been able to successfully raid on the old Republic bases or caches that remained scattered throughout what once had been Republic space.

Food wasn't the only problem that the taskforce was facing though. Ordinance was quickly becoming an issue as well. Despite the four ships among the taskforce that had the equipment to manufacture more missiles and other armaments, the *Pickman* was left with only fifty-five percent of the amount of armaments she should be carrying. If she was that low, how many other older ships were likely close to being completely unarmed? He couldn't just contact all the other captains to feel things out without Admiral Powell coming down on him and accusing him of conspiring to bring about a full-scale mutiny. The worse things got for the taskforce, the more the good admiral seemed to grow paranoid that he was out to get him. There were indeed a good number of captains who would love to see the admiral's head on a pike, but he wasn't among them. All he wanted was for the insanity to end and he kept telling himself that eventually even Admiral Powell would have to realize that the war against the Swarm had been lost for some time. If Taskforce Hope continued as it was, it would only be a matter of time until it was destroyed down to the last ship.

The door to his ready room opened as Allen entered. He could tell from Allen's expression that his XO brought more bad news.

"Am I interrupting you, sir?" Allen asked.

"Come on in, Allen, and have a seat," Harrison said, waving him on.

Allen entered and took a seat in one of the chairs in front of his desk.

"We're still processing all the supplies the transports that escaped from the *Laybourne* brought with them, but it looks like they were forced to leave a lot of key things behind. The few ship parts they did carry with them are a blessing, sir, but..." Allen paused.

"They didn't bring enough ordnance to speak of?" Harrison ventured.

"Well, that too," Allen admitted. "It's the lack of countermeasures that concerns me though. I saw you scanning over the reports as I came in. Did you notice that this ship has less than twenty percent of countermeasures she's supposed to be carrying to be considered combat capable?"

Harrison sighed. "No, I hadn't gotten that far yet."

"The next time we enter an extended engagement with a Swarm fleet..."

"We may find ourselves at the mercy of their missiles," Harrison finished for him. "I'll put in a request to the *Homestead*, but I think we both know what good that will do."

The mention of the *Homestead* caused Allen to shot him a nervous glance. "Have you heard anything more from Admiral Powell?"

Harrison's expression grew darker as he answered, "Not yet."

"You know he's not going to let what you did in Desmond go," Allen warned.

"The battle was lost long before he gave the order to disengage and withdraw. This ship and her crew are my responsibility." Harrison leaned forward. "Taskforce Hope has sacrificed enough lives to Powell's cause already."

"I am not saying I disagree, sir." Allen looked to be choosing his words with great care. "In fact, I agree completely, but Admiral Powell is in command of the Taskforce."

"I am well aware of that fact," Harrison sighed.

"You're playing a dangerous game, sir," Allen told him.

"It's not a game," Harrison corrected him. "Someone has to do what's right."

Allen had no reply. He fidgeted in his chair and cleared his throat before he spoke again.

"The crew of this ship is with you, sir," Allen said, "Whatever happens."

"Thank you," Harrison said sincerely. "Now don't you have some repairs you should be overseeing?"

Allen laughed. "I suppose I do, sir."

"Then get to them Allen and leave the worrying about Powell to me," Harrison ordered.

Harrison watched Allen leave before returning his attention to the reports he had been scanning through before his XO had arrived.

Allen had barely been gone five minutes with the comm. next to Harrison chimed.

"There's a shuttle from the *Homestead* requesting permission to come onboard, Captain," Claudia's voice informed him. He could tell from the concern in her tone that she knew as well as he did why the shuttle had been dispatched to the *Pickman*. As tempting as it was to order the shuttle blown apart, Harrison knew that the troops aboard it were only carrying out Powell's orders. Doing so would be murder and in the end, solve nothing.

"Grant them permission to come onboard, Claudia," Harrison instructed her. "Tell them I'll be waiting for their arrival in my ready room."

****

Lieutenant Wallace slammed a fist into the console of his Reaper. The sleek, fighter craft had taken a hit from a Swarm missile. It was a miracle he was even alive. The missile's detonation had damaged its canopy, and Wallace had been trapped inside the fighter for hours. The *Steakley*'s hangar crew was hard at work on getting him out, but his patience had reached its limit.

"Simmer down in there, son!" the hangar chief yelled at Wallace over the comm. in his helmet. "Hitting those controls is only going to cause me more work after we get you out."

Wallace kept his reply to himself. Two, very long minutes later, the welding torches finally cut through whatever keeping the canopy locked in place. Wallace leaped from the fighter as soon as the canopy was opened.

"That was a close call you had there," the hangar chief told him.

"I'm the only reason you're breathing right now, old man," Wallace snarled at the chief. "If I hadn't damaged that missile and then intercepted it, this ship would be a mass of debris."

The hangar chief glared at him. The man looked to be in his later fifties, and Wallace almost wished the chief would say just a little bit more to give him a reason to deck him.

Wallace's home carrier was the *Hellbringer*. He wanted desperately to be back aboard her, but given the state of his fighter, it looked like he was going to be stuck here for far longer than he liked. In essence, he had only traded one trap for another by getting out of his Reaper. The chance that he could con a transport or shuttle pilot to give him a ride home was slim at best. Non-essential traffic between the ships of Taskforce Hope was usually kept to a minimum even when the taskforce hadn't just blinked out of direct combat with the Swarm.

"Lieutenant!" a woman who wore the rank of captain on her sleeve shouted as she approached him.

Wallace snapped to attention.

"You will apologize to Chief Pierce right now for your behavior!" the woman ordered. Wallace couldn't help but stare at her. Her beauty took his breath away. She stood five foot seven, all toned muscle and fury, her flaming, red hair curving over the sides of her face in a bob cut.

"For what, ma'am?" Wallace asked.

"Your attitude, pilot," she told him. "If not for the chief and his men, you'd still be inside that pile of scrap over there."

Wallace ground his teeth. "Ma'am, do you know who I am?"

"You're Lieutenant Hunter Wallace from the *Hellbringer*," she answered, catching him off-guard. "Two hundred and fourteen sensor-verified kills as of this last engagement with the Swarm."

"Yes, ma'am," Wallace answered, swelling with pride.

"Know that we all know who you are, let me ask you this," she said. "Do you know what you are?"

"The best bloody Reaper pilot in Taskforce Hope, ma'am," Wallace answered.

"You're part right, Wallace," she chuckled. "You're a pilot and a lieutenant. I'm a freaking captain, so you're going to apologize to the chief here this instant, or I am personally going to see to it that your life is a living hell while you're aboard this ship."

Wallace was taken aback by the redheaded captain's grit. Usually, his rep caused folks to cut him some slack. This captain didn't give a crap who he was or what he had done. Part of him respected her for that but only a small part. Looking at her, Wallace had no doubt she would toss him in the brig if it came to that.

"Sorry for any disrespect, Chief," Wallace said to the old man.

Chief Piece grinned at him. "No worries, son. I've been around pilots long enough to know that most of you are crazy, have to be to take the chances you do out there, I guess."

Wallace chuckled. The old man's answer made him smile. He relaxed some and turned to the captain. "I'm sorry, ma'am," he said without promoting.

The redheaded captain returned his smile extending her hand. "Captain Mary Steadman. Welcome aboard the *Steakley*. I suppose I'm your new C.O."

Wallace gaped at her in disbelief.

"You don't have to look so stunned, Wallace," she told him.

"Sorry, ma'am," he blurted out then tried to get himself together. "About returning to the *Hellbringer...*"

"Non-essential flights are out while the taskforce is conducting repairs, Wallace. You're going to be stuck with me for a while I'm afraid. I realize you have to be a bit high strung right now given that you were almost blown to hell," her grip was firm as he took her hand and shook it, "but like I said, I've read your file. One would think you'd be used to it more by now."

"Maybe I am more rattled that I thought," Wallace admitted.

"Pilot ready alert barracks are that way." She pointed down the hangar towards a distance door. "Get some rest if you can, but know that if the Swarm comes gunning for us here, I expect you back in space with the rest of us."

"My Reaper..." Wallace started to protest as it would be a long time until his fighter would be spaceworthy again if the *Steakley*'s hangar chief didn't just decide to scrap it for parts.

"I don't know how things are on the *Hellbringer*, Wallace, but here on the *Steakley*, pilots are what we need, not Reapers. This carrier had a Swarm fighter come burning it all kamikaze-like, guns blazing, into the starboard hangar bay a few months ago. Took out over half of us. We've drafted replacements of course, but they're newbies with little experience. Having a pilot like you suddenly at my disposal is a gift from God."

"I'm not a babysitter, ma'am," Wallace said. "I'm a killer."

"You're both now, Wallace," Steadman said firmly, leaving no room for argument.

****

Captain Harrison stood as Colonel Chero entered his ready room. Two, full combat gear marines in the elite battle dress of *Dealers* accompanied him. Dealers were Admiral Powell's personal, internal security forces who dealt with any issues inside the taskforce that arose. They were given the power to deal out whatever justice they saw fit, on the spot, on a case-by-case basis. Harrison had heard stories of Dealers ordering offenders to their knees and executing them with a bullet to the head before God and everyone present without any regard for anything or anyone beyond their orders.

Two members of the *Pickman*'s own security teams started to follow Colonel Chero and the Dealers into his ready room. Harrison waved them off. They were brave men and he felt pride at their loyalty to him, but if things went south, they'd just end up dying too and he didn't want their blood on his hands when it didn't have to be. Colonel Chero watched his dismissal of the two security officers and nodded his approval.

"I had heard you were a man of reason, Harrison. It's good to see that it's true." Colonel Chero smirked at him and took a seat in front of his desk without waiting to be offered it.

Harrison sat down behind the desk across from him as the two Dealers remained standing behind the colonel.

"I trust you know why I am here," Colonel Chero commented.

"Admiral Powell isn't happy with how I conducted myself during the recent engagement with the Swarm," Harrison stated the obvious.

Colonel Chero raised his hands, interlocking them and popping his knuckles before settling down to business. "Yes, but we're here for more than that, Captain."

"Last time I checked, free speech was still legal." Harrison tried to keep too hard an edge from his voice.

"Taskforce Hope is under martial law, Captain," Colonel Chero reminded him. "I'd think a man like yourself would do well to keep that in mind."

"I've committed no crime," Harrison stated flatly.

"You ordered this ship to prepare for blink when no such general order was given," Colonel Chero corrected him, wriggling a finger in his direction. "That gets me to wondering if you were about to make a run for it, Captain, and if it makes me uneasy, well, then you can imagine how Admiral Powell feels about it."

"Issued an order for the fleet to disengage and withdraw within moments of me giving that order to my astrogation officer," Harrison responded.

"That's beside the point." Colonel Chero grinned in a manner that showed Harrison his overly white teeth. "You know that too, Captain. The admiral can't have the commanding officers of his fleet endangering us all."

It was getting harder for Harrison to keep his feelings in check. "I think what you mean is Admiral Powell can't stand the thought of anyone challenging his authority."

"As the commanding officer of Taskforce Hope, Admiral Powell's authority is absolute in all things." Colonel Chero produced a thick cigar from the pocket of his jacket and lit it up.

The smell was nauseating to Harrison, but he knew complaining about it would only make his situation worse.

Colonel Chero leaned forward in his chair and blew smoke at Harrison. "You have two choices, Captain Harrison, and I think you know exactly what they are. Which is it going to be?"

The Dealers behind the colonel tensed their gun hands flexing at their sides as they awaited his answer.

"I have no personal issues with the admiral," Harrison explained. "Never have. However, I am responsible for this ship and the lives of her crew. If the admiral really wants you to haul me in for acting in their best interest, then you're going to need to cuff me, Colonel, and get it over with."

Colonel Chero plopped his cigar between his lips and leaned back in his chair, steepling his fingers in front of him. Several heartbeats passed in silence before he replied, "It's not quite gone that far yet, Captain Harrison, but this will be your final warning. If you see me again, I won't be cuffing you to back to the *Homestead*. You'll be promptly dealt with wherever I find you."

"I understand," Harrison answered.

"Be sure that you do, Captain Harrison. It's not very often my boys get to deal out justice to officers of your rank, and I would hate to see it happen to you. It would really be a waste as badly as Taskforce Hope needs men and women with your combat experience and talent."

Colonel Chero rose from his seat. "Good day then, Captain Harrison. I'm glad we were able to have this talk in such a rational and civilized fashion. These are my favorite boots I am wearing, and blood does have such a nasty tendency to stain things."

The door to the ready room slid closed in their wake as the colonel and his men left. Harrison ran the backside of his hand across his brow to wipe at the sweat there. He had been lucky and he knew it. Next time, there wouldn't be any discussion; his blood would be splattered all over the walls and floor.

****

Admiral Powell felt much better after the four hours of sleep he had gotten. Colonel Chero had returned from his visit with Harrison and assured him that the matter with the strong-headed captain had been dealt with and was well in hand. Chero seemed convinced that Harrison would fall in line now. Powell wasn't so sure, but he wasn't ready to order the execution of an officer as capable as Harrison yet. For all his personal faults, Harrison was among the best ship captains Powell had under him. The man's tactical assessments and instincts rivaled his own. To make matters worse, the bulk of the *Pickman*'s crew were as loyal to the man as his Dealers were to him. If the matter was handled poorly, there was a very good chance that the *Pickman* would be lost along with Harrison if push came to shove.

Putting the matter aside, Powell commed for coffee to be delivered to his quarters as he took a seat at the small workstation near his bed and fired it up. He brought a three-dimensional image of the star system around the one where Taskforce Hope was currently making its post-battle repairs into being. He stared at it, trying to figure out where the Swarm would be weakest within their current striking distance. If Spinner's new virus panned out, there was no need for Taskforce Hope to fight its way deep into Swarm space to deliver it to the bugs. Any target with a large enough population would do so as long as there were survivors who unknowingly carried the virus to the rest of the Swarm in the battle's aftermath. Of course, Spinner had told him it would be weeks, at least, until the virus was viable, and Taskforce Hope couldn't remain here that long. Doing so would be like an open invitation to the Swarm to blink into the system and tear them apart. Taskforce Hope had to move.

That left him with two options. He could move the Taskforce around from one unoccupied system to another and try to steer clear of the bugs until the virus was ready or after the current repairs were complete, he could hit another target. There was plenty of time to do so and still be able to prepare for a second assault afterwards that he hoped would the final one Taskforce Hope would face from a position of being outnumbered and outgunned. Spinner's data suggested the virus, once delivered, would sweep like wildfire throughout the Swarm fleet, killing most, if not all, of the bugs very quickly. The trick with the virus was going to be delivering it somewhere that its spread wasn't outpaced by its mortality rate.

Powell began to closely look at each displayed star system in turn as he copied the data he was looking at and forwarded it on to Dr. Spinner, accompanied with the order for Spinner to select a system that would work for the dispersal of the virus. Spinner was better suited to pick the target system for the virus to be let loose in. In the meantime, Powell wasn't about to waste time the Taskforce could be using to keep the Swarm off balance in preparation for their real strike against the bugs.

The Yogotha system appeared to be very promising. There were Swarm shipyards there and very little in terms of a battlegroup to defend them. Taskforce Hope had been zigzagging its way along the boundaries of Swarm space, hitting any target they could. The Swarm had to know the Yogotha system could be a target for them. Even so, the system's shipyards were defended by no more than a single super dreadnought and a small compliment of battleships with their destroyer screens. In all, the system's defenders numbered less than three dozen total ships. Part of that lack of defense could be due to there being no Swarm colony in Yogotha. It was purely a military system. The presence of the super dreadnought could be a factor in its lack of other defenses as well. Swarm super dreadnoughts were rare. The Swarm had only begun constructing such ships after their contact with the Republic and learning of their existence. Oh, they had Hive ships even back then, but they were mainly carriers, not the potential fleet breakers/planet killers like this one clearly was based on the *Homestead*'s long-range scans. Powell believed that the Swarm must think that the presence of the super dreadnought was deterrent enough to keep Taskforce Hope from making a move against Yogotha. He was about to prove them wrong. Powell shutdown his workstation and rose from his seat with a grim, almost feral smile stretching his lips.

"Yogotha," Powell said the system's name aloud. He left his quarters with a determined stride. There were plans to be made and much work ahead now that he had his next target.

****

Ashley stood at attention between Elliot and Weston. All ten members of the Helldogs squad had assembled for an out-of-the-blue inspection and briefing. Lieutenant Clarkson, her new CO, looked to be slightly younger than she was. Ashley didn't think of herself as old. She was only twenty-six, but in Taskforce Hope's infantry, age was a relative thing. She felt ancient even though she knew she wasn't. Over the last two years, she had seen more than her share of death and the horrors of war.

She noticed the lieutenant was staring at her. If the kid was trying to get her riled up or intimidate her with his rank, he really did have a lot to learn about being in the infantry. Weston had told her this was Lieutenant Clarkson's first command. He was fresh out of the taskforce's version of the academy and it showed.

Ignoring his other troops, he marched up to stand directly in front of her. "Trooper, what are you smirking about?" he growled in her face.

Ashley hadn't realized she was smirking until the young lieutenant had called her on it.

"Nothing important, sir!" she barked at him.

"Do you know why you're here, trooper?" Clarkson shouted.

"To kill bugs sir!" Ashley answered.

Clarkson nodded apparently pleased enough with her answer.

"Word has come down from up top that we'll be seeing some heavy action soon." Clarkson grinned.

Ashley figured if the kid knew what heavy action was really like, he wouldn't be grinning about sent into it.

"Admiral Powell has a plan that should bring an end to the Swarm once and for all."

Never heard that before, Ashely found herself smirking again.

"And the Helldogs are going to play a big role in that plan," Clarkson continued. "How many of you know what a mech is?"

Ashley heard Elliot groan beside her.

"It's like bigger, more complex power armor, sir," Weston barked.

Mech technology had been in development for decades, constantly being designed and redesigned. The Republic had fielded mechs on numerous occasions during the early days of the Swarm War, but every time they had failed to live up to the powerhouses they were supposed to be. More often than not, the mechs are too slow. It made them walking targets. All the armor and firepower in the world didn't matter if the enemy concentrated their fire on you and you couldn't get out of the way. No amount of armor could hold out forever, especially not with every bug that was in a position to take a shot at it pouring their fire into it.

"Are you telling us that we've just become armored troops, sir?" Elliot spoke up.

The young lieutenant whirled on him. "Who told you that you could speak, trooper?"

The glare Elliot gave Lieutenant Clarkson was a sharp contrast to the words that came out of his mouth, "Sorry, sir!"

The young lieutenant seemed to calm some. "But yes, the Helldogs have just become an armored squad." Clarkson stabbed a button on the wrist comp. he wore and the wall behind him slid open to reveal eleven mechs. Each of the machines stood nearly ten feet tall. Their thick armor was painted in the swirling, darks hues that Ashley recognized as those one often saw inside a Swarm battleship. Not very many soldiers had ever boarded a Swarm ship and came back alive. She and Elliot were among those lucky few who had come back.

Each of the mechs had an auto-cannon in place of a right hand at the end of that arm. Otherwise, the mechs resembled squat, burly human forms.

"These are the Helldogs Mark I," Lieutenant Clarkson explained. "Fresh off the production line."

Ashley saw that Elliot just couldn't help himself as he raised his hand like a kid in a classroom to get the young lieutenant's attention.

"Yes, Trooper Elliot?" Clarkson said with an edge of exasperation.

"Mechs have never worked before, sir," Elliot told him. "What makes you think these will be any different?"

"These Helldogs have all new synaptic interfaces that will tap directly into our nervous systems, exponentially increasing their reaction times. In addition, though they look much like the older classes of mechs, they're not. Their joints have been redesigned as has their power system to make them almost as agile as an unarmored trooper."

"Believe it when I see it," Elliot whispered to her as Ashley sighed.

"And how much time to do we have to train in these, sir, and get used to their interface?" Ashley asked.

Lieutenant Clarkson actually frowned. "That's the bad part, trooper. We've got a few weeks tops. But we're Helldogs, Oorah!"

"Oorah!" all the Helldogs, herself and Elliot included, shouted.

"We'll be starting training at oh six hundred," Lieutenant Clarkson informed them all. "Make sure you get some rest before then. You're going to need it."

****

Hunter Wallace sat in the ready alert barracks of the *Steakley*'s port hangar bay. It was late, and though he had managed to catch

31

a quick nap, he was exhausted. He had a Stem with two doses left in it inside the lining of his flight suit but wasn't ready to use it yet. Stems could have some pretty adverse effects, and he had seen enough pilots get hooked on them to know that overusing them was trouble.

There were five other pilots waiting with him. Most of them were playing cards at a nearby table, and the other one was zonked out in a bunk despite the noise of the game. There was no sign of Captain Steadman. So far, she was the only interesting thing he had seen about the *Steakley*. The *Steakley* was an older ship than his home carrier, the *Hellbringer*. The paint of its walls was flaking. Its age was his real issue with the carrier though. It was the laidback, relaxed state of its pilots and hangar crew. Aboard the *Hellbringer*, everything was so much more intense. Everyone was always ready for the next battle of the war to start. These folks on the *Steakley* almost acted as if they were on a pleasure cruise in comparison. It got on his nerves.

With each passing hour, the odds that the Swarm was going to come gunning for the Taskforce in this system went down. Wallace had accepted that he likely wasn't going to be climbing back into the cockpit of a Reaper tonight. The odds of the Swarm finding Taskforce Hope would swing the other way as time passed, but for now, they were in what he typically thought of as the middle safe-zone.

The other pilots he shared the ready alert barracks with had gone out of their way to include him, but he had rejected those efforts. Most of them seemed awestruck by who he was. To them, he was a living legend in the flesh. His answers to their annoying, fanboy questions were short and cold.

The atmosphere aboard the *Steakley* just wasn't what he was accustomed to being from the *Hellbringer* even without their fascination with him. Eventually, they had realized at last that he wanted no part of them and moved on, which was fine with him. Wallace had always been a loner. He had learned a long time ago that the only two things you could count on in life and combat were yourself and your Reaper.

He wasn't looking forward to breaking in a new fighter when the time came. Every Reaper had its own quirks and idiosyncrasies just like a person did. Learning those little glitches in its systems was essential if you wanted to be able to push the fighter to its max and beyond. The Reaper that was likely about to be scrapped for parts by the old man that was the *Steakley*'s hangar chief had been his for over six months. She had taken a lot of fire but had always been able to be patched up before. Wallace was going to miss her.

The other pilots in the room stopped what they were doing and rose to their feet as Captain Steadman suddenly entered the ready alert barracks.

"At ease." She waved them back to their seats. "This isn't an inspection."

Wallace sipped at the cup of cold coffee he cradled in his lap where he sat near the rear of the barracks and smiled at her. She returned his smile as the other pilots went back to their game, though he noticed they stole glances when they could at the captain and himself.

Captain Steadman took a seat near him. "I can tell you're fitting in just fine."

Her voice dripped with sarcasm.

"These boys here, they know when to leave a man alone, I'll give them that," Wallace told her.

"The chief has officially declared your Reaper a pile of junk." Steadman frowned. "Sorry about that."

Wallace shrugged. "I expected as much."

"You're a cold one, Wallace," Steadman commented.

"Have to be," he answered.

"Not all the time," Steadman said. "You may be a legend, but you're still human. Look around you, Wallace. These guys know they're going to go out there sooner or later and they may not come home from it, but—"

Wallace stopped her there, "Look, I don't need a lecture on living life and all that crap. If that's what works for you, fine. That's your thing. You guys here can pretend that we're not at war with an enemy that kicked our collective butts a long time ago. You can pretend that this Taskforce still has a future that isn't a fiery death. Me? I'm not going to pretend. I'm going to focus on my job and get it done right up until the end finally comes."

Steadman raised an eyebrow. "That's certainly disappointing to hear," she said.

Steadman rose from her seat, standing over him. "You're a hero to a lot of people in this taskforce, Wallace. Maybe you should start acting like one."

With that said, Captain Steadman exited the barracks without another word to him or anyone else. Wallace watched her go, his gaze locked onto the sway of her hips. For a Grade A witch, she was hot. Wallace reclined in his chair and let his mind wander into some very fun places.

****

Admiral Powell called a meeting of Taskforce Hope's top captains aboard the *Homestead,* the taskforce's only super dreadnought and flagship. Captain Steadman from the *Steakley,* Reece from the *Hellbringer,* Hyatt from the *Nomad,* Rigel from the *Weber,* Torel from the *Centurion,* and Harrison from the *Pickman* were in attendance. They represented the best that Taskforce Hope had at its disposal. Powell hadn't been sure that Harrison would attend given his recent insubordination and visit from Colonel Chero's Dealers. He was glad Harrison had come though. Best to keep one's friends close and one's enemies closer he supposed. Besides, having Harrison here gave him a chance to appraise him up close and see personally just how much of a danger he might be.

"The Yogotha system will be our next target," Admiral Powell informed them all, calling into existence a three-dimensional representation of the system and its shipyards above the center of the conference table.

The representation showed the sprawling mass of Swarm shipyards between the system's third and fourth planets. It also depicted the forces protecting them. A single super dreadnought accompanied by a force of Swarm battleships sat in space near them. Destroyers moved about the system on patrols. In all, the Swarm ships in the system numbered around three dozen.

Captain Steadman spoke up, saying what Powell was sure the others were thinking. "Admiral, that's a super dreadnought."

Powell nodded. "Yes, Steadman, it is, and I understand your concern."

"Admiral, Taskforce Hope can't afford to risk taking on that level of firepower, can we?" Captain Torel asked.

Harrison laughed darkly from where he sat at the other end of the table. Powell glared at him.

"We can if Admiral Powell is willing to risk the *Homestead*," Harrison said.

Powell could see the shock on the faces of the other captains.

"It's a risk we need to be willing to take," Powell responded. "Every ship in this fleet is running low on…just about everything. If we can take those shipyards intact, imagine what we can take from them. Fuel, the raw materials for more munitions, further repairs our ships, even food stuffs. Not all of what the Swarm race consumes is incompatible with our own biology. Taking those shipyards would give us what we need to continue on for some time."

"I can't argue that," Harrison said with a sly grin, "but the last system was even less defended than this one. What makes you think the bugs won't blink in reinforcements just as fast here?"

"The super dreadnought," Torel jumped in. "It's there for a reason."

"Torel's right." Steadman nodded. "It's rare we see one at all these days. If they have one assigned here, it could mean that they expect it to be this system's protection and don't have ready ships to blink into it."

"I tend to agree with that assessment as well," Hyatt said. "Despite the shipyards, there's nothing else in this system for the bugs to protect. It may just be that the defenses we're seeing are indeed the only ones on ready alert for Yogotha."

"Even so, we're still talking about a super dreadnought!" Rigel almost leaped from his seat. "And that's not even considering the fleet with it."

"We outnumber the Swarm forces nearly three to one even with our recent losses." Admiral Powell smiled. "If the *Homestead* directly engages the super dreadnought, she can certainly hold it long enough for the rest of our ships to deal with its accompanying fleet then it's just a numbers game."

Powell cleared his throat before continuing to let his words sink in. "Super dreadnought or no, we can take the Yogotha system."

"But we could never hold it," Harrison pointed out.

"We wouldn't need to," Steadman said. "We'd just have to take what we need from those shipyards quickly and get out. Pretty standard procedure there. We've raided targets just as large in the past and survived."

"Are we really this desperate?" Harrison asked. "If we lose the *Homestead*, Taskforce Hope is doomed. It might take a while, but without her, life in these ships just isn't indefinitely sustainable."

"It never has been," Rigel said. "We all know we're living on borrowed time. Each day we're alive is a miracle in sense."

"Perhaps I need to make myself clearer," Powell growled. "I didn't bring all of you here to discuss whether or not we're hitting Yogotha but to prepare for doing so. We need to come up with a plan on how to best blink into the system and eliminate the enemy as quickly as possible. I'll expect each of you to have a plan for doing so to me within eight hours."

All the captains stared at Powell. Harrison and Reece appeared angry. Steadman merely looked concerned. As to the others, they seemed to have fallen in line just as he had expected them to.

Before there could be any more discussion on the matter, Powell snapped, "You're dismissed. Get back to your ships and get me those plans."

He watched the group of captains leave, frowning as he did so.

****

Reece caught up to Harrison as he was about to board the shuttle back to the *Pickman*.

"Hey, Harrison!" Reece called after him.

He turned and waited for Reece to reach him.

"This plan of Powell's is insane," Reece said quietly.

Harrison gave him a cautionary look. "This is Admiral Powell's ship. You sure you want to have this discussion right now?"

"You know as well as I do that he has folks monitoring all the fleet's comm. chatter. Here is aa good a place as any." Reece shrugged.

"I'm already on his list, Reece," Harrison said. "Colonel Chero and his dealers paid me a visit before the meeting."

Reece's eyes bugged with shock. "It's come to that, has it?"

"Afraid so." Harrison shrugged. "Powell and I have never seen eye to eye, and the worse things get, the more that becomes clear to him, I suppose."

Reece shifted about on his feet. "Well, damn…"

"You watch yourself, Reece," Harrison warned.

"You really mean that, don't you?"

Harrison nodded. "I think Powell would already have me in the brig or worse if he could."

"The other captains would never stand for it," Reece said. "I know I wouldn't."

"Those are big words, Reece. Let's hope we never have to test them."

"This plan though…"

"Orders are orders, Reece." Harrison frowned. "Powell has made up his mind. We're going to hit Yogotha no matter the risk or the cost."

"He's going to get us all killed," Reece said.

Harrison shrugged again. "Maybe not. Either way, all we can do is get ready for it and fight like Hell when the missiles start flying."

Reece nodded. "I just thought…"

"What?" Harrison asked. "That I would stand up to him, save us all? I'm not a hero, Reece. Besides, like I said, I'm already on his list. You can bet I'm being watched and now you likely will be too."

Reece looked around the hangar, his eyes scanning for Dealers or anyone who might report what had just been said. He looked scared out of his mind.

"Get back to your ship, Reece," Harrison told him. "Your crew is going to need you."

****

After its repairs were completed, Admiral Powell had ordered Taskforce Hope to blink into a system in better striking range of Yogotha. He wanted the entire Taskforce to be able to blink into Yogotha in a single blink. Captain Steadman had told Wallace all about the admiral's plan and he helped her come up with the battle plan she had submitted to the admiral. Her plan had been rejected. Neither of them knew whose plan the admiral had decided to run with, but they knew its details, and that was why Wallace had been pushing the pilots of the *Steakley*'s fighters so hard. Five days had ticked by since he had joined the *Steakley*'s crew. It was difficult to believe that much time had passed, but Captain Steadman had kept him busy ever since her meeting with Powell. He had never been a teacher before and was surprised at how naturally he had slid into that role under Steadman's orders. Her pilots were making good progress towards his standards, but they weren't ready for what they were headed into and Wallace knew it. He figured Steadman knew it too. She joined him on patrol and in the exercises he was putting her pilots through as often as she could. If she had her way, Wallace figured she would be right there with them when the time came. She couldn't though. As the carrier's captain, her place would be on its bridge, watching over them from there.

They hadn't slept together yet, but Wallace knew he was letting his guard down with her and he couldn't help it. There was just something about Mary that got to him on a deeper level than just her looks.

"Shouldn't you be in your Reaper?" Captain Mary Steadman asked as Wallace entered her ready room just off the *Steakley*'s bridge. "We're less than an hour away from the blink into Yogotha."

"Headed there now." Wallace grinned. "Just wanted to check in and see how you were doing."

She looked frazzled and Wallace didn't blame her. She was about to jump her ship into combat. Neither of them was overly happy with the plan that Admiral Powell had settled on, but there was nothing they could do about it. At least, Wallace thought, the *Steakley* would be out of the main line battle. The *Steakley* was a carrier so she, the *Hellbringer*, and Taskforce Hope's other non-combatant ships would be bringing up the rear. In truth, there was no such thing as a non-combatant ship anymore in the war with the Swarm. Taskforce Hope often had no choice but to travel as a whole. That meant putting all its ships at risk, but the only option was to leave the manufacturing ships, etc. alone and unprotected. If the Swarm stumbled onto them before the taskforce's warships returned, that would be game over for humanity.

The *Steakley* was by no means unarmored or unarmed. She had been built for combat, but she wasn't a battleship. The amount of pounding she could take was limited. Her job was to merely bring her half of the taskforce's Reapers into the battle and resupply them as needed.

"How do you think I am doing?" Steadman laughed, shaking her head.

"Better than I would be in your place," Wallace said honestly. Command wasn't his thing and never would be. He was too much of a loner.

"I imagine Rigel never gets flustered," Steadman said.

Rigel was the captain of the *Hellbringer*, the taskforce's only other carrier. He was also Wallace's real C.O. Rigel was a hardcore, militant commander whose style of command was utterly different than Steadman's. Until he had become stuck on the *Steakley* after the last battle with the Swarm, Wallace had thought Rigel was the best captain Taskforce Hope had. Now, he wasn't so sure. There was something to be said for the more human approach Steadman took in her command, where everyone was important and everything wasn't always decided by need or rank.

Wallace shook his head. "Not really, but then you have other things going for you."

"Such as?" Steadman asked, leaning forward in her chair with keen interest in her eyes.

"Rigel's pretty fixed in his ways, ma'am. You're much more open-minded. With Captain Rigel, everything's black and white. You can see the gray though."

Steadman smiled at him and then changed the subject. "Are my new pilots ready?"

"You want the honest answer?" Wallace asked.

She nodded.

"No, but they're as ready as they can," Wallace told her.

"That will have to be good enough then," Steadman sighed. "Thank you for what you've done for this ship, Wallace. I know I came down on your pretty hard when you first arrived, but I think you needed that."

"I think I did too," he admitted.

Silence stretched between them as they stared at each other for a moment.

Steadman was the one to break it. "You better get to your Reaper. The clock is ticking."

"See you after," Wallace promised as he saluted her then left her alone at her desk.

****

"Two minutes to blink," Captain Harrison heard his XO, Allen, announce.

"Mr. Boyes?" Harrison asked his helmsman.

"All systems green and ready for blink, sir," Boyes responded.

"Sound action stations," Harrison ordered.

"Action stations!" Allen barked over the *Pickman*'s internal comm. "Shields up!"

Harrison drummed his fingertips on the arm of his command chair as he watched the clock tick down. Taskforce Hope was jumping into Yogotha in a single, simultaneous blink. Once in the system, the taskforce would be dividing up into seven groups – six attack groups that would charge headlong into the enemy forces awaiting them there and a seventh group of non-combatant ships that would be pushing their engines to escape the heat of the battle and withdraw a safe distance from the main conflict. Each of the six attack groups was assigned preselected targets based on long-range scans of the Yogotha system and under the command of one of the elite captains of the Taskforce. Harrison's group was designated Battlegroup II. Admiral Powell was leading Battlegroup I aboard the taskforce's only super dreadnought, the *Homestead*. If the *Homestead* was destroyed, overall command would fall to him. That fact surprised him greatly given the bad blood between himself and the admiral. However, Powell knew that he was the taskforce's best hope for survival even through his madness and paranoia.

"And three...two..." Allen started the final countdown as Harrison stopped drumming his fingertips and gripped the arms of his command chair tightly.

"One... Blink!" Allen shouted.

Space bent around the *Pickman* and the ships of Taskforce Hope. The *Pickman*'s forward view flashed with the light from the blink and then all Hell broke loose.

Harrison saw the formation of Swarm ships spring into existence on the viewscreen.

"All ships, Battlegroup 2, concentrate fire on the Swarm battleships!" he ordered.

He figured they could worry about the Swarm destroyers later. The Swarm battleships were the real threat.

The *Pickman*'s forward launchers spat volley after volley of missiles towards the Swarm ships as her railguns concentrated their fire on a single Swarm battleship. The Swarm battleship must not have had time to come to full alert and raise its shields because the *Pickman*'s railguns cut deep slashes in its forward armor.

"We've caught them with their pants down, sir!" Allen shouted.

"Bugs don't wear pants," Harrison said though his attention was focused on the battle. The various battlegroups of Taskforce Hope had broken apart and were heavily engaged with the Swarm ships. It did appear they had caught the bugs completely by surprise. The Swarm ships own formation was breaking up as well under the taskforce's fire. There was no order to their maneuvers. Their reaction to Taskforce Hope's sudden arrival resembled a mad scramble to get the hell out of its way. In the chaos, Harrison watched as two Swarm destroyers, both trying to evade the taskforce's fire and position themselves to better return it, collided with each other. The ensuing explosion was magnificent and lit up the darkness of space.

"Swarm ships returning fire, sir!" Allen warned as the first waves of Swarm missiles from the ships his battlegroup was engaged with came streaking towards them.

The *Pickman*'s countermeasures came online. Battlegroup 2 outnumbered their portion of Swarm ships by almost four to one. The Swarm ships hadn't concentrated their fire either; instead, each of them firing at its own target. The *Pickman*'s ECMs alone sent a third of the missiles coming towards her spiraling away into the void, their targeting systems scrambled. Her point defense guns made short work of the others. Harrison relaxed a bit in his command chair, but he knew such luck couldn't hold, even in a battle as lopsided as this one appeared to be.

Harrison kept a close eye on the status of the other ships of his battlegroup through the AI of his command chair. The *Bontee* was the only ship in Battlegroup 2 that had taken damage thus far, but the damage it had taken had been severe. A Swarm destroyer, in a desperate attempt to screen the battleship it accompanied, had opted to ram the *Bontee*. The *Bontee* barely survived the collision; its shields were knocked offline and a large section of its hull was smashed open. The Swarm destroyer was now little more than a debris field in the *Bontee*'s wake.

Harrison started to order the captain of the *Bontee* to withdraw, but before he could, a volley of missiles from a nearby Swarm battleship finished her, tearing her apart in a series of explosions that rippled from her stern to bow. There was no time to mourn the loss. The *Pickman* had her own problem.

One of the Swarm battleships came sweeping towards the *Pickman*, its close-in energy weapons blazing. The *Pickman*'s shields glowed bright underneath the near point-blank fire.

"Evasive maneuvers!" Harrison shouted at Boyes.

The *Pickman* rolled in space as she twisted herself out of the Swarm ship's line of fire. She returned fire with a volley of missiles that gutted the Swarm battleship, nearly cutting it in half.

****

Admiral Powell had thought he was ready as Taskforce Hope blinked into the Yogotha system. War was his life. It had consumed him since the moment he had assembled Taskforce Hope in the wake of the Republic's death. Yet now, he stared in at the ghastly image of the massive Swarm hive ship on the *Homestead*'s forward viewscreen with an edge of fear. A long time had passed since his flagship had gone one on one against a super dreadnought class Swarm vessel with the end of fighting it head on to the death. He glanced over at the *Homestead*'s captain, Robinson, who basically served his XO. Robinson appeared to be keeping his cool and getting the job done.

"Fire all forward weapons!" Robinson roared.

The other five battlegroups of Taskforce Hope were cutting a swath of death through the Swarm ships in front of them as they should, considering their advantages in numbers and of surprise. The Swarm battleships and destroyers which hadn't already been dealt with were in utter chaos and not fighting as a unit but rather merely trying to do what damage they could before they too met a fiery death.

The *Homestead*'s initial wave of missiles were hammering the Swarm Hive ship's shields as it brought its own weapon systems online and returned fire. Beams energy arced through the space between the two massive ships striking the *Homestead*. They danced and weaved over its shields.

"Mr. Robinson!" Admiral Powell shouted, leaping from his command chair to his feet.

"Shields are holding!" a bridge officer cried.

Powell saw Robinson shoot him a worried glance as the *Homestead*'s railgun emplacements opened up on the Swarm Hive ship. The Hive ship had closed inside of the super dreadnought missile range. She couldn't fire missiles now without taking damage from them herself.

"Get us out of here!" Admiral Powell ordered.

The *Homestead*'s drive spiked in power, straining to back the super dreadnought away from the Hive ship as its energy beams continued to rake over her shields. The Hive ship moved forward, keeping its weapons at full against the super dreadnought's shields.

"Fire forward missiles!" Admiral Powell told Robinson.

"But, sir!" Robinson protested, "Our shields…"

"That was an order, Robinson!" Admiral Powell spat.

Every forward launcher of the *Homestead* erupted simultaneously. The two massive ships were so close that the time from launch to impact wasn't even a full two seconds. The *Homestead*'s forward viewer went white as over two hundred missiles detonated against the Hive ship's shields. The Hive ship's shields crumpled beneath the fury of the blast and sections of its forward armor caved inward. Atmosphere leaked from the fractures. The *Homestead*, however, felt the blast as well.

Admiral Powell dropped back into his command chair as the bridge beneath his feet rocked. Alarm klaxons blared through the *Homestead*.

"Damage report!" he heard Captain Robinson shouting.

"Shields are down. There are reports of hull breaches and causalities coming in from all over the ship!" a crewman answered.

"We've lost most of our forward missile tubes and railguns as well, sir!" another crewman called out.

Admiral Powell looked up to stare at the image of the Swarm Hive ship on the forward viewer. It looked in pretty rough shape. He imagined that the bug that was in charge over there was thinking much the same about the *Homestead*.

The Hive ship's forward movement had come to a halt so the *Homestead* was pulling away from it, her drive continuing to push her backwards. The Hive ship's energy weapons came to life again in the wake of the explosion. Their fire was less intense, but this time, the *Homestead* had no shields to lessen the damage they caused. Arcs of lightning like energy slashed at the super dreadnought, cutting into her already-weakened forward armor and cutting new paths of metal melt along her hull.

"We got to stop that thing!" Robinson yelled. "We can't take much more of this!"

The *Homestead* couldn't afford to launch another barrage of missiles at such close range or she would be destroyed along with the bug vessel. That left only what few railguns that were still functional to return fire. They blazed away at the Hive ship, spewing continuous streams of fire into it, but Powell could see it wasn't going to be enough. The amount of damage they were inflicting was nothing compared to what the Hive ship's energy weapons were doing to the *Homestead*.

****

The moment the *Steakley* had blinked into the Yogotha system, a dozen assault shuttles rocketed out of the hangar bays of the *Pickman* ahead of her. The *Steakley* launched sixty of her Reaper class fighters to accompany them. The Reapers took a defensive formation around shuttles shielding them from any missiles that came their way. Those were few and far between as the attention of the Swarm ships was focused on the massive fleet of Taskforce Hope that had just blinked into existence in front of them. Wallace's new Reaper was among them.

Their target was the sprawling mass of the largest shipyard that lay beyond the group of Swarm ships trying to desperately to protect them. Wallace checked the streams of scrolling sensor data displayed on the interior screen of his flight helmet. While he wasn't really worried about incoming fire from the Swarm warships, the shipyards themselves were powering up their own weapons.

"All Reapers prepared for evasive maneuvers! The bugs aren't gonna let us get in close without a fight!" he ordered. "Tango 2, Tango 3, you're with me. Concentrate fire on the primary docking doors just below the southward battleship that's under construction. We need to clear the way for those shuttles to get in and drop their cargo!"

Even as he gave the order, he gripped the firing controls of his Reaper's auto-canons and activated them. Streams of automatic rounds streaked across the darkness of the void to hammer into the section of shields that covered the docking doors. Fire from Tango 2 and 3 joined his own. All three Reapers kept their fire constant as they rocketed towards their target. The shields shimmered under the assault and finally gave way.

The shipyards' weapons lashed out at the incoming Reapers and shuttles. They put a few missiles into space that were quickly taken out by the lead Reapers. Their real defense though was their close-in beam weapons. The inbound Reapers had no defense against those other than luck and the skills of their pilots. Several of the energy beams that arced outwards made contact with the Reapers they targeted. Those fighters disintegrated, instantly blown apart. Reapers had no shields and their armor was next to nonexistent. The one-man fighters were built for speed and to deal out damage, not to take it.

Wallace flinched as out of the corner of his eye he saw a Reaper move up to intercept a blast of energy that had been meant for the trio of Reapers he was leading towards the shipyard's primary docking doors. That pilot had given his or her life to keep Wallace's detachment intact.

"Break!" Wallace screamed, jerking his own Reaper upwards at the last moment as he neared what was left of the shipyard's docking doors. The concentrated fire from himself and his two companions had done the job and not only broken through the shipyard's shields there but reduced the doors to a mangled mass of jagged metal. As his Reaper angled to where its underside faced the hull of the shipyard and he flew upwards above the target his auto-cannons had cut to shreds, he looked back to see the first of the assault shuttles ram its way through the mangled doors and into the shipyard's dock. The other shuttles would follow it in soon enough and be on their own against whatever awaited them inside the shipyard. He had gotten them to their target and opened it up for them. His job with the shuttles was over. Now what he had to worry about was getting the *Steakley*'s Reapers, himself included, back aboard her in one piece.

****

Ashley's Helldog had its own inertial dampening systems. Even so, she was jarred about inside the massive suit of power armor she piloted as the shuttle carrying it rammed through the docking doors of the bug shipyard. Weston's Helldog crouched beside hers in the rear of the assault shuttle. Their two suits clanged against each other as they bounced about. The assault shuttles were designed to carry normal troops to their target, not power armored ones. As thus, each shuttle could only fit two suits in its rear and that very tightly and awkwardly so. She wished Elliot were with her, but he was aboard another shuttle like the one she and Weston were in. He'd be joining her soon enough, but it was up to her and the newbie to lead the charge into the shipyard's docking area. The shuttle carrying her and Weston had been forced to come in hot, ramming through the remnants of the bay doors in order to gain entrance to the shipyard's interior. She felt the impact as it slammed into one of the dock's interior walls and its flight was brought to an end with the sound of crunching metal.

There was no time to wonder if the shuttle's pilots had survived. She kicked her Helldog suit into gear. It rose from its crouch, knocking the rear door of the shuttle from its path. The door went flying outwards into a group of armed bug warriors who were already racing towards the downed shuttle. It struck them head-on, sending them sprawling onto the docking bay floor. Ashley never gave them the chance to recover and get to their feet. Her Helldog leaped from the shuttle's rear in the door's wake, the barrels of the auto-cannon that was its right hand spinning. They hosed the group of bug warriors with a barrage of high-velocity rounds that cut them to pieces where they lay.

Weston followed after her, his Helldog's auto-cannon targeting another group of bug warriors approaching from their right flank. The body of the group's leader jerked and spasmed as the rounds blew its arms from its shoulders and reduced the exoskeleton of its chest to pulp. The other bugs surrounding him took their share of hurt as well. The black pus-like ooze of bug blood splattered everywhere as Weston's bullets ripped into them.

The sensor suite of Ashley's Helldog warned her of hundreds of other bug warriors all around the docking bay as a second assault shuttle came through the wreckage of the dock's doors. Unlike her's and Weston's, it was able to touchdown properly before the two Helldogs it carried emerged from its rear.

Bug soldiers, like bug warships, used mainly energy weapons. They carried bizarrely shaped rifles that resembled twisted worms in their pincer-like hands of their upper set of arms. Their lower set of arms ended in human-like hands, with six fingers each. Those were used for more delicate work than carrying and firing their strange energy rifles. Ashley knew full well how deadly a prolonged blast from those rifles could be even against a mech like the Helldog she piloted. She didn't intend to let the bugs get the chance to use them though. Ashley planned to keep them off balance enough until the rest of the Helldogs were aboard the shipyard and they could start their push into its interior together.

Ashely swung her auto-cannon back and forth, not aiming so much as laying down wild cover fire, as she sprayed the entire area of the dock in front of her.

"You planning on killing them all yourself there, young lady?" she heard Elliot laughing over her Helldog's comm. He had been on the second shuttle to enter the dock, and his Helldog was sprinting across the bay join her where she stood.

All but one of the shuttles had touched down now and eight of the ten Helldog mechs had been deployed inside the shipyard's docking area. The last shuttle had just entered the bay and was about to land when a thick spike of crackling orange energy sliced into its port side. The spike tore completely through the shuttle, leaving a massive hole behind it. The shuttle was flung sideways in the air before it exploded in a rain of shrapnel and flaming debris.

Ashley spotted the two bugs hoisting a huge, RPG-looking weapon between them. She knew at once that was where the energy spike that which destroyed the shuttle had come from. She whirled around, bringing her auto-cannon to bear on the two bugs. They fell before its fury, their blood splashing onto the docking bay wall behind them.

"That was the LT's shuttle!" Weston cried out. From the sound of his voice, the newbie on the edge of utterly freaking out.

"Calm it, kid," Elliot told him. "You're running with the big dogs now. Ashley and I ain't gonna let anything happen to ya."

Good play, Ashley thought. Elliot knew what a big deal the kid thought she was. For once, her rep might actually do some good.

"All Helldogs, advance!" Ashley shouted over the unit's shared comlink. She didn't bother telling the others she was assuming command; she just took it and led them on into the shipyard.

They had lost their advantage of surprise and the bugs were beginning to get it together. Scores of energy blasts smacked into the Helldogs and bay around them. Energy melted metal where it hit. Ashley's Helldog caught only a single bolt as she threw herself to the right, dodging most of the bug's fire by ducking beneath the bulk of a docked bug shuttle. That bolt sliced a deep groove in the left arm of her suit but not deep enough to compromise it. The atmosphere of the Swarm shipyard was breathable to humans. She had breathed bug air before. It stank of sulphur but only long-term exposure to it was harmful. As long as their promised infantry reinforcements arrived within the hour as they were supposed to, they'd all be fine, even if any of their suits got breached. The Helldogs' job wasn't to take the entire shipyard alone but rather merely to secure a beachhead in the shipyard's docking area for the rest of Taskforce Hope's troopers to deploy.

A grim smile stretched across her lips as she leaned her Helldog around the corner of the bug transport she was using as cover and opened fire at the bug warriors on the other side of the bay again.

****

Captain Harrison's mouth fell open as the *Pickman*'s sensor tech yelled, "Two Swarm fleets have blinked in system!"

Harrison had expected something like what was unfolding around him all along but had hoped he was wrong. Admiral

Powell may very well have killed them all this time if things played out as he suspected they would.

"Disposition of enemy vessels?" Harrison shouted.

"Each fleet contains a Swarm Hive ship at its center, sir," the sensor tech reported. "Each is accompanied by an additional three dozen battleships."

"God help us," Allen muttered.

Harrison's fingers danced over the keys of the arm of his command chair as he accessed the sensor feed himself, scanning the Swarm Hive ship's energy emissions.

"They're triangulating their power," Harrison said to Allen.

Allen stared at him in disbelief and shock.

"They're creating a blink jamming web around Yogotha." Harrison frowned as his stomach lurched and he felt as if he was going to throw up.

"With just three ships?" Allen asked.

"Those are Hive ships, Allen," Harrison explained. "They can do it."

Allen shook his head. "What do we do?"

"Not much," Harrison said. "Get me Admiral Powell! Now!" he snapped at Claudia.

"Yes, sir!" she answered. "Hailing the *Homestead* now!"

Harrison watched her struggling with the controls of the communications station.

"The *Homestead* isn't responding sir!"

"Damn it!" Harrison raged, slamming a balled-up fist down onto the arm of his command chair.

"We've got to blink out before it's too late," Allen urged him. "To Hell with Powell's orders!"

Harrison's eyes were glued to the sensor data he was watching on the small screen of his command chair. "It's already too late," he told Allen.

Allen went white as Harrison shook his head. "We're in this one to the end, so let's make dang sure we go out in a blaze of glory."

The *Pickman* and its battlegroup had already laid waste to its assigned portion of the already in-system Swarm battleships and had been on course to aid the *Homestead* as per Admiral Powell's orders. Harrison had a choice to make. He could have the *Pickman* continue on that course, because if the *Homestead* was lost, there was little chance of the rest of Taskforce Hope surviving in the long run, or he could bring the *Pickman* about and go charging towards the new Swarm ships that had just entered Yogotha. If he could hurt one of the other Hive ships badly enough, he could take down the anti-blink energy web that they had cast over the Yogotha system so that Taskforce Hope could blink away and make a run for it.

"What is the status of the *Homestead?*" he asked his sensor tech.

"She's taken a lot of damage, sir," the tech replied, "but she's holding her own."

Harrison rubbed at his chin with the fingers of his right hand thinking it all over.

"Helm, bring us about," Harrison ordered. "All ships of Battlegroup 2, prepare to engage the Hive ship to port. Maximum military speed!"

****

The *Homestead*'s bridge was a disaster. The continued hammering of the super dreadnought by the wounded Hive ship's energy weapons had done a great deal of damage. His own tactic of launching a point-blank barrage of missiles into the Hive ship hadn't helped things either, and the combined damage of the two had hurt the *Homestead* greatly. The lights of the bridge glowed red as they had switched over to emergency backup power. All of the super dreadnought's drive was being channeled into reinforcing its structural integrity and keeping it moving away from the wounded Hive ship that continued to try to close in on it.

Causality reports and reports of hull breaches continued to come in from all over the massive super dreadnought. Captain Robinson was doing all he could and Admiral Powell knew it, but that didn't change the reality that if the super dreadnought wasn't able to fully breakaway from the Hive ship it was engaged with or help didn't arrive, they'd all soon die.

Where in the devil was the Pickman? Admiral Powell wondered. Harrison was under strict orders to come to the *Homestead*'s aid as soon as his section of Swarm battleships had been dealt with. Comms were down. The *Homestead*'s chief engineer assured Powell that he would have the comm. systems back online and functional within a matter of minutes. Minutes though in a space battle like this one could be the difference between life and death though.

"Robinson!" Admiral Powell called.

The ship's captain, who basically acted as the admiral's XO, turned to him. "Sir?"

"Do we have a location on Battlegroup 2?" Powell raged. "Are they inbound?"

"Admiral," Robinson told him. "Two more Hive ships have blinked in Yogotha, sir. They've brought with them a good number of other reinforcements as well. Battlegroup 2 was in route to assist us when those forces appeared."

Powell gritted his teeth, almost snarling at Robinson as the captain continued to explain what had happened.

"Upon the arrival of the new Swarm forces, Battlegroup 2 altered course to engage one of the new Hive ships and its accompanying fleet."

Admiral Powell started to let loose a litany of curses damning Harrison to Hell, but before he could, the arcs of crackling energy from the Hive ship that the *Homestead* was engaged with once again managed to tear a gaping hole in the *Homestead*'s forward hull. The super dreadnought shook as the rupture formed along its front and portion of the bridge ceiling above Robinson caved in. Captain Robinson never even had time to scream. One second he was there, and the next he had vanished beneath a pile of debris on the bridge's floor. Bright red leaked out around the corners of the pile of debris.

There were panicked screams all around the bridge. Another station blew out as a power surge ripped through it. The poor girl at the shields station was engulfed in flames as the console she sat at exploded in a shower of sparks and flames. She rose from her seat, the entire top half of her body ablaze, wailing like a banshee. Powell drew his side arm and shot her through her forehead. Her body toppled to the floor with a thud.

"Get it together, people!" Powell ordered. "We either win this one or we all die! It's time to stop screwing around and kill that Hive ship out there before it kills us!"

****

Ashley and the remaining Helldogs were hunkered down behind two docked Swarm transports. They had been unable to push their way deeper into the shipyards and were taking a heavy beating. Four of her Helldogs had been taken out already, and there was no sign of the infantry support that should have arrived some time ago.

"What the hell is going on?" Elliot asked her over the comm.

"I don't have a fragging clue!" Ashley snapped at him as she took a shot a bug warrior with the auto-cannon of her Helldog suit. She hit the bug warrior with enough rounds to reduce it to an explosion of black blood and shattered bits of exoskeleton. Two more bugs came running up to take its place their strange energy rifles sending crackling bursts her way.

"You're the commanding officer, Ashley!" Elliot reminded her.

"That was the LT, Elliot, not me," Ashley answered as she ducked back behind the edge of the docked bug transport. The fire from the two bug warriors ripped away at it but didn't penetrate the shuttle to reach her. "He was in command, remember?"

"Doesn't matter, kiddo. You are now. What the hell are we supposed to do?" Elliot yelled over the sound of the battle raging in the bay.

There was no means of getting off the shipyard. The shuttles that had brought them in were toast. As what was supposed to be a quick entrance and charge deeper into the shipyard had turned into a prolonged battle that had led to the Helldogs getting pinned had continued, each of the shuttles had been systematically taken out by the bugs. The bugs had paid a steep price in blood to do so, but they still managed to destroy or cripple all the shuttles.

A warning alarm beeped inside Ashley's Helldog drawing her attention to the fact that her auto-cannon was down to twenty percent in its magazine. "Ammo is becoming an issue," she said aloud over the comm.

"Really?" Elliot chided her. "I never would have guessed!"

A Helldog to Ashley's right took a hit from a bug energy rifle. The blast burnt a hole clean through the mech's head and exited its backside. The Helldog froze for a second, its auto-cannon extended towards the bug warriors its pilot had been aiming for, and then crashed sideways onto the floor of the docking bay. Ashley knew its pilot was dead without even bothering to check the status readout on her command display.

"We can't stay here, Ashley!" Elliot warned her.

"Elliot, unless you see something I am missing, there's nowhere we can run to!" she shouted back at him. "The bugs have got us surrounded!"

"I think it's time to accept that help ain't coming," Elliot told her.

"We don't know that, Elliot!" Ashley argued.

"Yes, we do," Elliot growled.

"We've just got to hold on a little while longer," Ashley said.

"Screw that, kiddo! We've got to get out of here!" Elliot said after a moment. "I'm going to clear the way!"

"Elliot!" Ashley screamed as she saw his Helldog rise from behind its cover and start running towards the largest mass of bug warriors who were blocking the bay doors that led into the shipyard's inner corridors. "Stand down!"

She knew Elliot could hear her but the stubborn bastard wasn't listening. His Helldog's legs pumped beneath its hulking, armored form, building up speed as it plowed towards the mass of bug warriors. Elliot's Helldog was taking heavy fire from every bug that had an angle of fire that allowed it to get off a shot at the charging mech. Parts of Elliot's Helldog melted away. Its entire right shoulder was slagged. Other shots tore chunks from its legs. Even so, somehow, Elliot kept the mech moving.

"Elliot!" Ashley screamed again, but her scream was in vain. Elliot's Helldog crashed into the mass of bug warriors, plowing into their ranks like a charging quarterback then it exploded. The power of the blast from the mech's overloading power source forced Ashley to dive deeper behind the shuttle she was using as cover. The explosion shook the entire section of the docking bay and brought down a good portion of its ceiling. When she was able to get a look at the damage Elliot's sacrifice had caused, she saw that he had indeed cleared the way. Most of the bugs were dead. Charred pieces of broken exoskeletons littered the bay floor.

"All Helldogs!" Ashley shouted. "Forward on me!"

Ashley led the other Helldogs out from behind their cover, running towards the entrance to the shipyard's interior. The Helldogs, herself included, kept firing as they ran, their auto-cannons chattering at full power. Elliot had cleared away the bulk of the bug warriors, but there were still more scattered around the bay.

She never saw the two bugs manning a huge, energy cannon between them on her left flank. The spike of energy the cannon spat burnt through the armor of her Helldog and cooked her alive inside of it.

****

Captain Mary Steadman held tight to the side of the *Steakley*'s helm as the entire carrier ship shook again. The *Steakley*, like the other non-combatant ships of Taskforce Hope, had steered clear of the engagement between the taskforce's warships and the Swarm fleet that had been in Yogotha when the taskforce had blinked in. Two more Swarm battle fleets, each including a Hive ship, had blinked into the system though. One of them had popped into existence right behind the group of non-combatant ships and opened fire on them.

The *Steakley*'s shields had failed within the first few seconds of the barrage of fire that the new Swarm fleet was pouring out. Even so, she was far luckier than her sister carrier, the *Hellbringer*. The massive Hive ship in the center of the new Swarm battle fleet had taken the *Hellbringer* out with a single blast of its primary energy weapon array. The other taskforce ships around the *Steakl*ey peppered the void with explosions of light and heat that reminded Steadman of fireworks she seen on Earth as a kid.

"We're at full power, ma'am!" Larkin, her helmsman told her, as Captain Steadman regained her balance. "The bug ships are just too fast for us to break away!"

Captain Steadman knew Larkin was right. The *Steakley* was a carrier. She wasn't exactly built for speed. Her mind raced searching for a means to escape the bug ships that were barreling down on them.

"Any luck restoring the shields?" Captain Steadman shouted across the bridge at her chief engineer.

The chief shook his head. "They're done for. Ain't nothing short of a complete overhaul gonna fix 'em!"

So far, the *Steakley* hadn't even tried to return fire against the new Swarm battle fleet chasing it. Captain Steadman hadn't bothered giving an order to do so. The *Steakley*'s weapons weren't going to do squat against a bug Hive ship, and engaging the battleships surrounding it would just tick off their commanding officers and make her even more of a target of the bugs' fury.

"Scramble every Reaper left aboard and start getting our combat shuttles into space too!" Captain Steadman ordered. "Then give the order for the rest of the crew to abandon ship."

"Yes, ma'am." Her XO nodded and moved to make her orders a reality.

"Incoming!" the young tech at the sensor station cried out. "Missile contact in one minute!"

"How many?" Captain Steadman asked, surprised to hear they had even that long.

"'Over two hundred, Captain!"

"Counter measures!" she yelled, knowing full well with that number of missiles inbound, they were dead already. She wasn't giving up though. "We have to stop those missiles before they reach us!"

The *Steakley*'s ECMs crackled to life. Several dozen of the bug missiles veered away from the *Steakley,* a few even turning to ram into the ones next to them as the *Steakley*'s close-in point defenses joined in. Hull-mounted railguns swirled on their turrets to engage the inbound missiles. Their streams of fire sliced into the missiles' ranks, destroying dozens more.

"Brace for impact!" Captain Steadman screamed as the fastest of the bug missiles began to strike the *Steakley*'s hull. The carrier swung sideways in space from that initial wave's impact. The next wave ended her.

Captain Steadman and her bridge crew died instantly as a random missile shredded the ship's hull above them.

****

Wallace and the surviving Reapers under his command were in route back to the carrier when the two new bug battle fleets had blinked into Yogotha. He watched in horror as one of those new battle fleets swept in on Taskforce Hope's non-combatant ships. Wallace poured on the speed, pushing his Reaper's engines beyond the redline, but it still wasn't enough. The *Steakley* blossomed in a growing orb of orange flames before he was halfway to her

"Mary!" he screamed as he watched the carrier die. Wallace closed his eyes and did something he hadn't done since he was a boy. He said a prayer, one for the soul of Captain Mary Steadman. It helped find his center again. When he opened his eyes, they were as hard and cold as they had been when he served aboard the *Hellbringer*.

The comm. chatter of the other pilots was full of fear and panicked voices. Some pilots were crying out to God for help. Others were swearing vengeance against the bugs. Most though were just trying to figure out what the devil they were all supposed to do. With both the *Steakley* and the *Hellbringer* gone, they had nowhere to run to. All of Taskforce Hope's battleships and its one super dreadnought, the *Homestead*, were all heavily engaged with the Swarm fleets. Even if they could reach one of them and get clearance to try a combat landing in a bay that wasn't really designed for Reapers, most of them didn't have the experience with their Reapers needed to try something that crazy.

Wallace wanted to continue on towards the Swarm fleet that had just wiped out a good portion of Taskforce Hope and sealed its long-term fate, but he knew the other pilots needed him. If he led them into the Swarm battle fleet, they might do some damage there. Not enough to matter though, he told himself. He'd just be leading them to their death and they deserved better than that. He had promised Steadman he would look after them and get them home. That wasn't an option now, but they were still his responsibility.

The *Homestead* was his best option. The super dreadnought was the only ship left in the fleet with bays designed for Reapers and it carried its own wing of them. From the looks of the sensor data his helmet showed him though, the *Homestead* wasn't far from being blown apart too. The Hive ship it had engaged upon entering Yogotha was continuing to chase it, pouring beams of crackling energy into it, as the super dreadnought looked to be doing its best to break away.

Any port in a storm, Wallace chuckled to himself darkly before he gave the order, "All Reapers, come about hard and make the *Homestead*. She's our ticket out of here!"

****

The *Centurion* and Battlegroup 4 had laid waste to their initial Swarm targets easily upon blinking into Yogotha and had then turned their attention to dealing with the Swarm destroyers that flitted about the outskirts of where the other Taskforce Hope battlegroups and the main Swarm fleet duked it out.

Captain Torel had figured things were going too well and sure enough, the bottom had fallen out of Admiral Powell's plan for taking the Yogotha system as two more Swarm battle fleets blinked into it. He had ordered Battlegroup 4 into a headlong charge towards the closest of the new Swarm battle fleets.

The *Centurion*'s forward railguns blazed as she sped towards the new Swarm fleet. Their fire raked over the shields of a Swarm battleship. The battleship's shields failed and the continued streams of fire tore long gashes across its hull. Returning fire, the battleship broke hard to port as two more battleships rushed forward to meet the *Centurion*. Captain Torel wasn't concerned. So far, the Hive ship hadn't engaged the *Centurion*. He knew that wouldn't last, but for now, it gave him hope that Battlegroup 4 could do some damage before it did.

The other ships of Battlegroup 4 found their own targets and took them on. The *Lemure* lurched as a volley of Swarm missiles ripped into her. The *Campbell* shot past a Swarm battleship, firing as it went. Explosions rippled along the Swarm battleship's length, glowing bright in the darkness of the void. A trio of Swarm battleships came at the *Garcia*, pounding her with a relentless volley of missiles that took out her shields and blew her apart in a matter of seconds.

The Swarm ship the *Centurion* was engaged with managed to get off a volley before her railguns finished it. The *Centurion*'s missile defenses stopped most of them, but a few got through. They hammered into her shields.

"Shields at fifty percent, sir!" Leo, one of Captain Torel's bridge officers, reported.

Captain Torel cursed under his breath in his command chair. He checked the scrolling feed of data on the chair's arm. The Hive ship was powering up its weapons. He was surprised the bug in charge of it had waited so long to join in the battle, then he saw why as he called up a close up view of the Hive ship. The tiny, bulges on its hull dropped away from it like flaking skin.

"Inbound bug fighters!" Captain Torel's sensor tech warned him.

"Ignore them!" Torel ordered. "Helm, take us towards the Hive ship. Concentrate all fire on its central energy weapon array!"

The *Centurion* turned, heading towards the Hive ship, her missiles tubes spitting one volley after another at the Hive ship. The inbound Swarm fighters reached her. They sped over her and along her length on strafing runs, their energy cannons blasting away at her shields.

"We've lost the *Campbell*!" someone shouted, but Captain Torel's attention was fixed on the Swarm Hive ship. It finally let loose with its energy weapons. Arcs of energy coalesced into a single spike that shot outwards to turn the *Lemure* into a flaming mass of wreckage.

"Sir!" Torel's XO called to him. "Our fire isn't getting through the Hive ship's shields! Should we break off?"

Captain Torel gnawed at the fingernail of his right middle finger. The old habit helped him think. As long as all three Hive ships were functional, Taskforce Hope was trapped in the

Yogotha system, unable to blink away. Somehow, at least one of the monsters had to be taken out.

"Ramming speed!" Torel ordered.

"Sir?" his XO asked, his eyes wide with the fear that clutches a person when they know they're about to die.

"You heard me, Lewis," Torel said. "Someone has to kill one of those Hive ships and we're in position to do so."

"Yes, sir!" Lewis nodded, accepting the *Centurion*'s fate and his own with it.

The *Centurion*'s speed increased as she streaked towards the Swarm Hive ship. If its captain saw them coming, he made no move to stop her. The Hive ship continued to fire at the other surviving ships of Taskforce Hope, destroying yet another Republic battleship for his efforts.

Torel smiled in the moment before the *Centurion* plowed into the front of the Hive ship. Flames erupted all over the bridge, and the *Centurion* exploded in a thunderous fury that took the Hive ship with her.

****

Aboard the *Homestead*, Dr. Spinner staggered into one of its larger docking bays. His lab coat was smeared with blood and one side of his face was badly burnt. Skin sloughed from it, revealing bone, as he raced towards the nearest shuttle crew loading up supplies to make a run for it. Word had come down that Admiral Powell was dead. The *Homestead*'s captain was dead too. Command of the massive super dreadnought had fallen some lowly lieutenant named Smith. The super dreadnought was still taking heavy fire, and every so often, the floor of the docking bay would heave, knocking those who weren't braced for it from their feet.

Spinner had received an automated message in his lab the moment that Admiral Powell had died. Its orders were to make sure the virus survived. Dr. Spinner, who typically never left the lab area of the ship, had found himself forced to grab what he could and go charging through the super dreadnought's corridors. The corridors were littered with the corpses of crewman smashed beneath collapsed internal walls and the wounded who had been trying to reach a medical bay but hadn't made it. Several times, he had been forced to change his course, going around sections of the ship that had been breached and sealed off by bulkheads that had slammed into place to keep the *Homestead*'s atmosphere from bleeding out. Each time that had happened, Spinner loosed a litany of curses that would have made the worst spacer blush. He was very aware of just how little time he had to save what he could and to carry out the admiral's final orders.

The group of crewmen loading the shuttle noticed his approach. One of them stopped loading supplies and rushed to meet him.

"Frag!" she blurted out as she saw how badly he was hurt. "How are you even standing?"

Dr. Spinner thrust the case he was carrying into her hands. "Take this. It's the key to our survival."

The woman accepted the case and clutched it tightly. He could tell from her expression that she knew who he was and just how important the case had to be.

"Get it off this ship!" Dr. Spinner screamed as her, blood flying from his lips. "You have to make sure it survives!"

The last of his strength gave way and he toppled forward onto his knees. The woman reached to help him, but he knocked her hand away. "The case, damn it! It's what matters, not me!"

The woman nodded and left him where knelt on the docking bay floor. Dr. Spinner watched her run up to the others around the shuttle, yelling to them about what he had told her.

Dr. Spinner lived just long enough to see the shuttle lift off and fly out of the docking bay into the stars beyond. He had done all he could to save his work. Its fate rested with a higher power now.

****

Captain Gerald Hall watched the last ship of Battlegroup 2 die. The *Pickman* had been destroyed only a few seconds earlier as she took two Swarm battleships with her. Captain Hall's ship, the *Magnum*, was an older class battleship, and he himself was far from one of Taskforce Hope's leading captains. He found himself in command of the few ships that remained of Taskforce Hope as the ranking senior officer left alive. That fact alone spoke volumes about how badly the taskforce had already been hurt during the Yogotha battle.

"Sir!" his XO, Grey, shouted at him. "The *Centurion* just took out one of the Hive ships! We can blink again!"

"Thank God!" Captain Hall exclaimed. "Spin up the Blink drive, and get us the hell out of here. Order all other remaining ships of the taskforce to do the same!"

"There's a Republic shuttle inbound for us, sir!" Hall's sensor tech yelled. "It's from the *Homestead!*"

Captain Hall wanted to curse but managed to keep his emotions in check and stay professional.

The *Magnum* was shaken as another barrage of Hive missiles finished her shields.

"Shields are down!" Grey reported.

"Order that shuttle to make a combat landing!" Captain Hall ordered. "And the second it's aboard, blink us out!"

"Where to, sir?" his helmsman spun to face him.

"I don't give a frag!" Captain Hall snapped from his command chair. "Just the hell out of here!"

"The shuttle is aboard, sir!" Grey told him.

"Blink!" Captain Hall screamed.

The *Magnum* vanished in a flash of light, leaving the Yogotha system and the ruins of Taskforce Hope behind her.

****

The system the *Magnum* blinked into was clear of Swarm ships according to the initial scans. Captain Hall slumped in his command chair, exhausted with sweat dripping from his brow. The *Magnum* was alone. If any of Taskforce Hope's other few surviving ships had gotten the coordinates Grey had sent them before the *Magnum* blinked out of Yogotha, they hadn't followed her.

Captain Hall wiped the sweat from his eyes and looked over at Grey who stood beside his command chair. "What the hell do we do now?"

Grey had no answer. The XO merely shrugged and said, "I guess that's up to you, sir. An equally valid question would be 'where are we?'"

Captain Hall agreed, but there were other things to be attended to first.

"Start repairs immediately," Hall ordered. "I want us ready if any Swarm ships show up here."

"Yes, sir." Grey nodded. "That sounds like a good idea."

"Also, start running long-range scans and see if you figure out where the hell we are," Hall said as he stared at the strange constellations of stars that filled the *Magnum*'s forward view screen. "And find out what was on that shuttle we picked up that was so damn important that shuttle was blaring priority alpha codes. I'll be in my ready room if you need me."

Grey moved to carry out his orders as Captain Hall got to his feet and addressed his bridge crew. "Good work, people. We may not have a clue where we are, and for all we know, we might be the last living humans left in this wretched universe, but keep in mind, we are alive. We have a future ahead of us still no matter what it might be."

Hall knew his little speech sucked, but it was the best he could manage. He staggered across the bridge towards his ready room, thankful to be alive, and determined to keep it that way. He plopped into the chair behind his desk, leaning forward to rest his head in his hands. In here, alone, he didn't have to hide what he was feeling. Tears formed in his eyes. He quickly wiped them away, embarrassed despite his solitude. Hall knew he had just witnessed the end of the human race. Taskforce Hope was gone, shattered by the Swarm. The war was truly over. Admiral Powell was dead. Captain Harrison was dead. The thought of Harrison stung him. The man had been his mentor when he had first taken command of the *Magnum*. Harrison had been more than just a mentor though. The two of them had grown to be friends in the year that followed. A year, it seemed like such a brief time now.

All those days vanished in a flash. All that time wasted fighting a war that had already been decided. Still, he remembered how proud he was when the taskforce's elite captain had chosen him to take command of the *Magnum* when her previous captain, Reid, had been killed in action. His hand slid the drawer of his desk open. Inside was perhaps the last bottle of vodka in the universe. He stared at before finally screwing off its top and pouring himself a glass.

For the life of him, he couldn't figure out why none of the other ships of Taskforce Hope had followed the *Magnum* here, to wherever here was. Yes, the blink coordinates had been random, but they been sent to all the surviving ships still engaged with the Swarm fleets before she had blinked out of the Yogotha system. Had they really *all* been destroyed? Had something gone wrong with the *Magnum*'s blink drive, plunging her somewhere completely different than where she had been meant to go? Hall supposed it didn't matter. Either way, the *Magnum* was alone. Her three-hundred crewmembers, and whoever had come aboard in the shuttle from the *Homestead* right before she blinked, could very well be the last of the human race. It was his job to keep them safe and figure out where they all went from here. And that was the problem, because he had no idea what came next.

****

Deck Chief Anna Pence stood in front of the still-smoking wreckage of the shuttle. It had come screeching into the *Magnum*'s port hangar bay during the final seconds before the blink out of Yogotha. Whoever the pilot was or had been was a good one. Though the shuttle had plowed into the hangar's wall, unable to stop its momentum, the pilot had managed to avoid damaging the other craft docked in the bay. Anna already had her crew working hard to get into the wreckage to see if anyone had survived the crash. So far, there had been no signs that anyone had.

The shuttle was a mess. Its forward section was crushed against the hangar wall, and its rear doors had been wedged shut somehow from the impact. Her crew was close to finally cutting through them. Sparks flew as their torches burnt away at the shuttle's rear doors. Anna heard the crack of the metal of the doors shifting and knew it was time.

"Get those doors off of there!" she yelled at her crew. Brent, a hulking man in his late twenties and one of her best workers, tossed his torch aside. Hamilton, who had been working with him, shut down his own torch and backed away from the shuttle to let Brent really get at it. Brent's gloved hands grabbed an upper part of the doors that held cooled some and yanked at it with all his strength. The door resisted his efforts at first, but Brent was determined to get through. He strained, grunting, as he jerked on the doors again. This time, the left door came loose from the shuttle. Brent hurriedly jumped out of its path as it clattered onto the floor of the hangar bay. Thick smoke rolled out of the shuttle's interior, but there was no clear sign of anything still on fire inside of it.

The two medics who had been standing by rushed forward entering the shuttle. All Anna could do was wait for them to re-emerge. Brent and Hamilton waited with her, worried looks on their faces. She knew Captain Hall wasn't going to be happy if everyone onboard it was dead.

"We got a live one," one of the medics called through the gas mask he wore as he stuck his head out of the shuttle. "Just one though, and she's barely hanging on."

"Damn it," Anna cursed under her breath.

"Do you need help getting her out?" Brent offered.

Anna smiled with pride. Brent might look like an oversized thug who could tear you apart with his bare hands, but the big man had a selfless heart like no one else she had ever known.

"Nah," the medic said, "We got this. Just get us a clear path to Med-Bay 1."

"You got it," Brent said and took off to clear a path for the medics through the other members of the deck crew who were standing around watching everything unfold. His voice echoed throughout the hangar as he plunged into them, barking orders and reminding them they all had work that they should be attending to.

The two medics came out of the shuttle, guiding an unfolded hover stretcher between them. On it rested a young woman. She wore the uniform of a marine. It was tattered and burnt. One of her legs was clearly broken, and the white of bone protruded through its mangled flesh. The left side of her face was little more than swollen and cooked meat. Most of her uniform was smeared with blood. Anna was sure that all the blood belonged to the young woman. There was just so much of it.

The two medics had placed an oxygen mask over her mouth and her nose. Anna could hear the young woman's pained moans as the medics rushed her past where Anna stood. It was then that Anna noticed the young woman was holding onto something with both her hands.

"What is that?" Anna stopped the two medics, pointing at the case the young woman was clutching so tightly.

"Don't know, ma'am," one of the medics told her. "She won't let go of it though, and given how bad she's hurt, we didn't force the issue."

Anna frowned. The case was briefcase-sized but made entirely of metal. That metal was cracked along the case's center and the entire case was carbon scarred from the flames that must been raging inside the shuttle at some point. Anna wanted to take it from the young woman. She didn't like unknowns. The case could be a personal item that the young woman was attached to or it could be something dangerous. The case had a definite military appearance to it. For all Anna knew, it could contain some type of explosives or a bomb. The young woman was a marine after all, and the shuttle had surely been loaded with whatever could be crammed onto it before it left the *Homestead*. Marines often put loading weapons and munitions above all else when they were bailing out from a ship that they knew was going to be destroyed by the Swarm. Anna needed to know what was in that case.

"Can you get it away from her?" Anna asked the two medics.

"Not without cutting off her fingers or risking her life in the struggle given the sort of internal injuries she likely has."

"Fine," Anna grunted. "Get it out of her hands as quick as you can though once she's in medical. I'll send Hamilton here to pick it up."

"Yes, ma'am," the medic nodded.

Anna watched the two of them guide the hover stretcher across the hangar and disappear into the *Magnum*'s internal corridors beyond it.

****

Peterson and Marshall guided the hover stretcher into the lift. "Med-Bay 1," Peterson told the lift's A.I. The doors closed and the lift shot upwards.

"I think she's trying to say something again." Marshall nodded at the young woman on the stretcher.

"Give her another hit of pain meds," Peterson ordered Marshall and leaned down to try to hear what the woman was saying. "What is it, Lieutenant?" he asked. Though her uniform was badly burnt and soaked in blood, he could still tell her rank from it.

The young woman's right arm snapped the restraints holding her to the hover stretcher as it shot upwards to grab Peterson by his throat. The force of her grip sunk her fingers into the flesh of his neck. Blood exploded from the crushed mess of Peterson's throat, splattering over Marshall and the walls of the lift.

Marshall was too stunned to react. His mind reeled at the sight of his partner's body toppling onto the floor of the lift as the young woman released him. Marshall wiped at the blood that had sprayed onto his cheeks, his eyes wide. He had heard of adrenaline giving people superhuman strength, but what the young lieutenant had just done to Peterson's neck was insane. He barely had time to react as she tore herself free from the rest of her restraints and lunged at him. He swung the pack of medical gear he was carrying up between the two of them just in time to block the balled-up fist that swung towards his face. The blow knocked the case from his trembling hands, denting its metal. The case the young woman had been holding to so tightly had clanged to the floor as she had sprung from the stretcher.

The lift was a tight fit for two men, a woman, and a hover stretcher. There wasn't much room to move about in, much less dodge the woman's fury. Marshall grabbed the end of the hover stretcher and yanked it between him and the young woman, trying to use it to keep her away from him. She gave an inhuman growl that chilled Marshall to the bone. Red foam bubbled upon her lips, her eyes full of murderous rage.

"Stay back!" Marshall yelled at her. "We were just trying to help you!"

She didn't seem to understand his words at all, or if she did, they didn't matter. It was clear that all she wanted was his blood. She took another swipe at him across the stretcher, but Marshall was able to fling his body to the side, dodging it. It was then he noticed her hands. Long, curved talons had grown out of her fingertips.

"God have mercy!" he cried as the lift reached the level Med-Bay 1 was located on and the door pinged open behind him. He leaped from the lift into the corridor outside it. There was a trio of crewman there, standing around waiting for the lift to arrive. He shoved into and through them as he screamed, "Watch out! She's insane!"

The woman followed out of the lift. She tackled the closest of the three crewmen, taking him to the floor beneath her. The man screamed and tried to throw her off of him, but she was too strong. Her head went down towards his neck as her teeth tore into the flesh they found there. A shower of blood erupted from the wound she had inflicted as she jerked her head back up, a chunk of the man's flesh dangling from her mouth.

None of the crewmen were armed, but that didn't stop them from diving into to try to help their friend. The largest of them wrapped his arms around the woman from behind her and yanked her into the air as the other rushed to the side of the man she had taken a piece out of.

"Help him!" the kneeling crewman cried at Marshall. "You're a medic, aren't you?"

Marshall ignored him, his eyes fixed on the big man who was wrestling with the woman. The woman had managed to twist around inside the big man's hold on her so that she faced him. He was screaming as her claws slashed at his face and shoulders, raking over them and leaving deep grooves in their wake.

The big man appeared to have had enough. She slung the woman into the wall of the corridor with a loud thud. The blow shook the woman but didn't knock her out. The big man took hold of her by the backside of her head and continued to pound her face against the wall. Marshall wondered if he was planning on killing her. It sure looked that way. Suddenly though, one of the woman's hands caught the big man's arm and snapped the bone inside of it with a sharp crack that Marshall could hear clearly from where he stood. The big man let her go, attempting to back away as he moved to cradle his broken arm. The woman didn't give him the chance though. She sprang onto him, sinking her clawed fingers into his eyes. Blood poured over the big man's cheeks in thick rivers of red. He was dead when she popped her fingers out of his eye sockets and he flopped to land at her feet.

The last of the three crewmen still knelt beside his friend who appeared to have stopped breathing. He leaped up to run at the woman, but with an effortless-looking backhanded swing of her right hand, she sent him falling into the corridor's wall. Marshall watched the man bounce off it and go rolling onto the floor.

By now, there were two more people who had heard the fight and came running to see what was going on. Marshall cursed as he saw that neither of them were security officers. The man and woman looked to be part of the *Magnum*'s engineering staff from the uniforms they wore.

Marshall waved from them to turn and head back the way they had come. "Run!" he yelled at them. "Get security!"

They must have gotten a look at the carnage littering the corridor outside of the still open lift because they did turn around and run like their lives depended on the speed of their legs. He ran after them.

Marshall knew he was dead the moment he felt the woman land on his back. She had jumped onto him from behind. The two of them crashed to the corridor floor. They rolled about as Marshall took hold the woman's wrists and fought to keep her claws away from his body. She snapped at him with her teeth like a rabid dog. Marshall flung his head from one side to the other, barely managing to keep her from taking a bite out of him.

At last, an armed security officer showed up. She came bounding down the corridor towards them, her gun drawn.

"Let go of him and back the hell away!" the security officer shouted. "I won't warn you again!"

"Shoot her!" Marshall screamed as he continued to fight with the woman on top of him. The claws of her left hand made contact with his cheek, slicing across it like razors.

The security officer opened fire. A carefully placed round blew the woman's right arm apart at her elbow joint. The severed part dropped to land beside Marshall's head as the woman shrieked and rolled away from him, springing to her feet. Marshall figured she would go after the security officer, but she didn't. Instead, she disappeared around the bend in the corridor as the officer took another shot at her. It blew a hole in the corridor wall, missing her completely.

The officer ran towards the corner of the corridor and took a look around it, her gun braced and ready in her hands.

"Where the hell did she go?" Marshall heard the security officer ask.

"She's fast," Marshall groaned as he rubbed at the shredded skin of his cheek. The wound there was burning.

"No? Really?" the security officer mocked him before she tapped the comm. piece she wore and started calling for backup.

****

Captain Hall shifted in the seat behind his desk as his XO, Grey, came bursting into his ready room.

"Sir!" the normally laid back XO yelled at him. "We've got a situation!"

Hall set his drink aside, meeting Grey's eyes. "The Swarm? Have they found us?"

Grey frantically shook his head. "No, sir. The shuttle that came aboard from the *Homestead*, it crashed during its combat landing. There was only one person that survived the crash, a young lieutenant by the name of Fran Wilson."

"And?" Hall urged.

"Two medics were transporting her to Med-Bay 1 when she went crazy on them, sir. Apparently, she killed one of them inside the lift they were using and then killed three more crewmen in the corridor outside it, sir, before a security officer showed up."

"Frag," Hall breathed. "Where is she now?"

"We don't know, sir," Grey admitted. "She got away from the security officer and was last seen on Deck 3."

"Bring the ship to alert status," Hall ordered. "Lockdown Deck 3. No one in or out until that woman is found. Do I make myself clear?"

"Crystal, sir," Grey nodded.

"I want that woman found and dealt with. Lethal force is authorized if taking her alive isn't possible," Hall paused. "Wait. You said she killed one of the two medics?"

"Yes, Captain," Grey said.

"What happened to the other one?" Hall asked.

"She clawed up one side of his face pretty badly from what I heard," Grey answered. "He's in Med-Bay 1 now having his wound treated."

Hall started for the door.

"Sir?" Grey stopped him. "Where do you think you're going?"

"Med-Bay 1," Hall answered.

"There's a homicidal lady running around out there, sir," Grey told him. "I don't think that's a good idea."

"Then get me an escort if you have to, Grey, but I am going to Med-Bay 1." His tone left no room for argument.

Grey tapped the comm. he wore. "Security to the captain's ready room. He needs an escort A.S.A.P."

That done, Grey took off to carry out the orders he had been given.

Though he hated every second of it, Captain Hall waited for two armed security officers to show up before he stepped out of his ready room. The three of them headed for the bridge's lift and entered it.

"Med-Bay 1," Hall ordered the lift as its doors closed.

"Don't you worry, sir," Fallada, one of the two security officers, assured him.

"You're safe with us," the other, Nicholson, added.

Hall kept his thoughts to himself as the lift lurched into motion.

****

Fran hid in the crawlspace of the maintenance shaft. Her breath came in a series of short, fast pants. She didn't know where she was or even who she was. Fran didn't care either. All that mattered to her was the hunger she felt. It was more intense than anything she had ever experienced. She longed for the warm, salty taste of blood upon her lips. Looking at the mangled stub of her left arm, she realized the pain from having it shot off her body was gone. The black stuff that her instincts told her was her blood had stopped flowing too. A new layer of purplish skin had grown over the wound, sealing it. She watched, astounded, as her arm began to grow back. The bone emerged through the layer of purplish skin first, extending from her elbow. Then flesh grew out of the bone to reform her arm completely. Fran flexed her new fingers, scraping the skin of palm with her long, claw-like nails.

Her teeth had fallen out of her gums and lay below her. Her tongue traced its way over the razor like, jagged ones that had replaced them. The glow coming from her yellow eyes was reflected on the metal of the shaft's metal. It was bright enough to light the enclosed space like a small candle.

Fran sniffed at the air. There were people close by. Both of them were male. She licked her lips at the thought of their taste. Fran crawled along the shaft, doing her best to keep quiet until she found a grate that looked down into an empty section of the corridor. Her clawed hands took hold of the grate, twisting its metal, as she ripped it out of her way and slid her body out of the shaft. Landing on her feet, her head jerked to one side and then the other. The men must have heard her leave the shaft. She heard their shouting voices approaching. She wanted to rush them but held herself in check, taking up a position at the bend in the corridor.

As the two men came charging around the bend in the corridor, their weapons held ready, she lunged onto them. Neither of them saw her until it was too late. Her claws tore at the first man's chest as she lifted him from the floor and tossed him into the wall like a ragdoll. The sound of his bones breaking inside of him was like music to her ears. The other man jerked up the pistol he clutched in her direction, squeezing its trigger, but Fran ducked the shot. It hammered into the wall behind her and she closed on the man, reaching up from under his arm, to tear the weapon from his grasp.

The man screamed, his eyes wide, as Fran's claws lashed out and plunged through his ribs into his heart. She ripped the still-beating organ from his chest and took a bite from it as the man staggered away from her. He made it two steps before his body realized it was dead and he toppled to the floor. A puddle of red grew about his body where it lay.

Fran took several more bites from the man's heart, savoring each, before she cast it aside. The other man was still alive. Though his body was broken, he was trying desperately to shift it just enough to reach the pistol that was on the floor next to him.

Letting loose a hiss of pleasure, Fran moved to kick the pistol down the corridor out of his reach. The man stared up at her as he begged, "Please. Please don't…"

Fran didn't give him the chance to finish his request. With lightning speed, she dropped onto him, tearing his nose from his face with her teeth. Hot blood sprayed over her and splattered the corridor's wall as the man struggled beneath her. As she swallowed what was left of his nose, she took hold of his head, the tips of her claws penetrating the bone of his skull and smashed his head back against the wall with such force it cracked open like a rotten melon. She wedged her fingers into the opening and cracked his skull the rest of the way open. Burying her face in his brain, she gnawed on it, swallowing entire chunks at a ravenous pace.

When she was done, Fran wiped blood and brain matter from lips with the back of her hand and rose to her feet. She sniffed the air again. The corridor and those close to it were empty of people, but her hunger was far from abated, despite her meal. She looked at the bodies of the two men. Now that they were dead, she had lost her taste for them. Fran needed someone else to feed on.

She reigned in the urge to kick her head back and cry out at the force of the hunger within her. Her yellow eyes blazed bright as, loping like an animal, she raced along the corridor in search of more prey.

****

"Don't look at me like that," Dr. Niles said to him as Captain Hall shot him a disdainful look.

"You know that smoking is the only thing that keeps me calm and functional," Dr. Niles snarled stabbing out his cigarette on the top of a tray of medical instruments.

"That can't be sanitary," Hall chuckled as Dr. Niles wiped at the blood staining his white medical coat with gloved hands.

"It's been a very long hour," Dr. Niles explained. "We were already on alert down here thanks to the battle with the Swarm, but none of us were expecting what your soldier boys brought in."

"And what did they bring in?" Captain Hall asked.

Dr. Niles shot looked at him as if he was an idiot. "You came all the way down here to pester me and you don't even really know what's going on?"

"I'm here to find out," Captain Hall grunted.

"Four dead people, that's what they brought," Dr. Niles spat. "Those poor souls were ripped up like some kind of animal had attacked them."

Captain Hall kept quiet waiting for Dr. Niles to continue.

"Screw it," Dr. Niles said taking off his gloves and digging a new cigarette from the pocket of his coat. He lit it and took a long drag from it before he spoke again. "I don't care what you think, Captain, this is my Med-Bay and I can smoke if I want to."

"The dead people?" Captain Hall pressed him.

"Yeah." Dr. Niles puffed out a cloud of smoke. "Someone or something really tore them up. They were all dead when they got here so there wasn't really anything I could do for them."

"The report I got said all four of them were killed by a young woman who came aboard on the shuttle we picked up from the *Homestead* just as we blinked out of Yogotha. I believe her name is Lieutenant Fran Wilson."

Dr. Niles snorted. "You're telling me you think one person killed all four of those men and a young woman at that?"

"Yes, I am, Doctor," Captain Hall said.

"Whoever killed those men captain, they were strong enough to do it with their bare hands at close range. If it was just a single woman, I want some of whatever she was pumped up on to give her that kind of strength. I've never seen anything like it. Do you know how much force it takes to sink your fingers *into* someone else's throat?"

Captain Hall shook his head.

"A hell of a lot." Dr. Niles kept puffing on his cigarette. "And if it was this young lieutenant as you saw, where in the devil did the claw marks on those bodies come from? They don't match any type of animal in our database, not that there should be any animals running around on this ship anyway. Did something come aboard with her on that shuttle?"

"Not that I am aware of." Captain Hall shrugged. "Like I said, the report claims she killed them all by herself, took a shot that blew off one of her arms at the elbow, and then managed to get away before security could restrain her."

"I'd like to see that arm." Dr. Niles was almost drooling at the thought of it.

"Security didn't bring it in?" Captain Hall asked.

"No," Dr. Niles answered. "They didn't mention anything about what happened out there. They shoved the bodies at us and disappeared like good, little soldier boys are supposed to do."

Captain Hall ignored the jab at his security personnel. He knew Dr. Niles hated anyone who carried a weapon to be used against another human.

"They did bring in something interesting though," Dr. Niles admitted, gesturing for Hall to follow him. Dr. Niles led him to a sealed glass square that contained a cracked metal case with the insignia of the *Homestead* on it.

"What is that?" Captain Hall asked.

"I was hoping you could tell me." Dr. Niles frowned. "According to Marshall, the medic that survived the attack, the young lady you claim is responsible for all the carnage I've just seen, was clinging to this for dear life when they removed from her from the wreckage of the shuttle from the *Homestead*. Damn thing set off every bio-alarm in here when they brought it through the door. We had to isolate it just to be able to turn the blasted things off. Whatever is inside of it must have leaked out to some extent when the case was ruptured."

"Do you know what was in it?" Captain Hall moved closer to the containment square.

"Best guess?" Dr. Niles shrugged. "Some type of bio-weapon. Those of us who work in medical have all heard rumors about the work Dr. Spinner was doing on the *Homestead*. Word was that the fool was cooking up a designer virus meant to wipe out the bugs."

"And you think that is what's in this case?"

"We're running tests to be sure." Dr. Niles finished his cigarette and dropped it onto the floor, grinding it out with the bottom of his shoe. "I'll clean that up when we're done, Captain but yes, I do. I do think Spinner's virus is in that case. There's no chance Spinner would risk it being destroyed with the *Homestead*. The guy spent the last two years of his life creating it."

"How long until you know more?" Captain Hall pressed.

"An hour or two, maybe." Dr. Niles frowned. "By then, I should at least be able to tell you what it is with certainty."

"Understood." Captain Hall nodded. "I want to know the second you do. In the meantime, just how dangerous could this virus be? Surely Spinner was working on a virus that affected the bugs not us."

"If Spinner screwed up or the virus mutated somehow, I'd say those four bodies that were brought in here, are an indication of just how deadly the crap in that case is. You need to catch that lieutenant from the *Homestead* and get her down here yesterday. If the virus is reacting with human biology, well, we could all be F.U.B.A.R.-ed already if it's airborne."

"What the odds of that?"

"I am sure Spinner's original virus had to be. How else could we have used it against the Swarm otherwise to have made a difference? But if it's mutated to affect humans, its vector could have changed too, and we better hope that it did because if it didn't, we're all likely infected already."

Captain Hall gritted his teeth against the helplessness he felt. "Just find out what you can as quick as you can and let me know.

Now, where's that medic that survived the attack? I'd like to have a word with him."

Dr. Niles pointed towards one the patient sections of Med-Bay 1.

"He's in bed four. Got him pretty sedated so good luck with chatting it up with him," Dr. Niles told him.

"I need him awake." Captain Hall watched Dr. Niles flinch at the force of his words. "Make it happen, Doctor. That's an order."

****

Captain Hall stood over the medic named Marshall. The wound on his cheek was bandaged but red pus seeped from beneath them to run over the medic's chin. Marshall and the bed sheets over him were drenched in sweat. Drops of sweat beaded on his forehead and even slicked his hands. Marshall's skin was pale.

"That's not normal, is it?" Captain Hall asked. "Did his wound get infected?"

Dr. Niles was shaking his head at the sight of Marshall. "No. None of this is normal."

"Nurse!" Dr. Niles yelled.

A middle-aged woman dressed in blue came running over to them.

Dr. Niles glared at her. "Rachel, what happened here?"

"I don't know, Doctor," Rachel answered nervously. "I followed your instructions about his care to the letter. He just started going downhill in the last few minutes. He had a mild fever when he came in, but it spiked. I've drawn fresh blood samples from him and sent them to the lab to be worked up."

"Why didn't you inform me?" Dr. Niles raged.

"I...I..." Rachel stammered.

"Forget it." Dr. Niles waved his hand dismissively. "Get me the data from some samples A.S.A.P."

"Yes, Dr. Niles," Rachel said and then darted away without looking back.

Dr. Niles picked up Marshall's chart and began scanning through it. Captain Hall remained quiet and let him do his job.

"This is insane," Dr. Niles exclaimed. "His immune system is in overdrive."

"What does that mean?" Captain Hall asked. "Can you still wake him up?"

"I don't think that would be a good idea," Dr. Niles warned. "I think we're looking at the early stages of whatever virus your young lieutenant brought aboard from the *Homestead*."

"So whatever Dr. Spinner cooked up over there does affect humans?" Captain Hall frowned.

"This man is proof of that, Captain." Dr. Niles matched his frown with one of his own.

Captain Hall could see that Dr. Niles was already forming a theory about the virus.

"Niles, I need you to tell me what you're thinking right now," Captain Hall ordered.

"I think, and this is just a theory mind you, that Dr. Spinner's virus is spread through bodily fluids, perhaps from scratches and bites from those infected as well," Dr. Niles told him.

"That's a pretty big leap without data to back it up," Captain Hall said, trying to sound like he knew what he was talking about.

"Oh, I think I've got some data right here." Dr. Niles waved Marshall's chart at him. "Not long ago, this man was perfectly healthy. Now, he's at death's door from nothing more than a scratch to his face."

"That's good news though, right? I mean, that this virus isn't airborne?"

"I didn't say it wasn't airborne as well," Dr. Niles said. "It could be airborne too and merely slower acting that way."

Captain Hall reached up with his right hand to rub at his mouth, crunching his lips together. The stress was getting to him and he was very well aware of it.

"Get me that lieutenant," Dr. Niles said. "She's the key to all this."

"Does it matter if she's alive?" Captain Hall asked and hated himself for doing so.

"Not at all," Dr. Niles answered.

****

"Hey, Sarge," Eibon shouted. "We got bodies over here!"

Sergeant Kaliner rounded the bend in the corridor, his rifle held ready, and stopped as he saw the two mutilated bodies that lay on the floor. Both of them were security officers under his command. He knew them by name.

There was blood everywhere. Charles' body was propped up against the corridor wall. His nose had been torn from his face and his skull cracked open. It looked like some animal had ravaged his brain. Derrick lay not far from Charles. There was a mangled hole in his chest. The white tips of broken ribs could be seen through it. Derrick's heart had been ripped from his body.

Kaliner noticed Derrick's heart on the floor nearby. Something had gnawed on it as well.

"What the hell are we hunting, Sarge?" Eibon asked. "I thought we were just after some woman that had gone crazy?"

"Me too," Kaliner admitted.

"No human could do this, Sarge." Eibon looked as if he was doing his best not to take a knee and throw up. Kaliner felt like doing that too. He'd seen a lot of death in his time but this…this was more than just death. This was open cruelty. Whoever had killed these men had fun with them as they took their lives and then stuck around long enough to eat part of them.

Kaliner tapped his comm. "Everyone rally on this signal A.S.A.P. Exercise extreme caution and stay alert. You see this woman we're after, take her out. Lethal force is authorized."

He had six more security personnel on Deck 3. Looking at Charles and Derrick, he knew that whatever they were up against, it was a lot more than they had thought they were dealing with.

Eibon kept glancing down the corridor and then back the way they had come.

"Really, I mean what the hell, Sarge?" Eibon complained.

Kaliner was continued to study the bodies. "Looks like she ambushed them as they came around the corner here. She was waiting on them."

"She is a trooper like us, sir," Eibon pointed out. "Apparently a dang good one too."

"It's more than that," Kaliner said. "Look at those guys, Eibon. She ain't a soldier anymore. She's something else now, and whatever it is, it isn't human."

Eibon stared at him as if he was crazy, but Kaliner ignored him.

Kaliner heard footsteps coming up towards the bend in the corridor behind them. He spun around, his rifle leveled at chest level, finger on the trigger. He did his best to stay cool and professional though he sure didn't feel it.

Dillon, Chris, Tim, and Paul rounded the corner.

"Whoa, Sarge!" Tim cried out. "It's us!"

Kaliner lowered the barrel of his rifle towards the floor. "Where are Michael and Chapman?"

It was Dillon who answered. "Don't know. Figured they must have met up with you already."

"Frag," Kaliner muttered.

"I'm guessing they didn't?" Tim quipped.

Kaliner typed into the arm comp. he wore calling the data on where he had sent the two of them.

"Beta sector," Kaliner said aloud.

"What?" Eibon who was standing close enough to hear him asked.

"I sent Michael and Chapman to secure Beta Sector," Kaliner said. "I bet that's where we'll find them and this Fran lady we're looking for too."

"You don't think –" Eibon started, but Kaliner cut him off.

"Everybody double time it for Sector Beta. Now! Tim, you have point!"

The six soldiers sprinted through the corridors of Deck 3 with Tim in the lead. Kaliner followed closely behind him with Eibon bringing up the rear.

None of them were ready when Fran dropped from maintenance shaft in the ceiling directly onto them. She landed in the middle of their formation, her clawed hands lashing out to slash across Dillon's eyes. Dillon howled as blood exploded from his face and he stumbled backwards into Chris, blocking Chris's line of fire. Fran snatched Paul, yanking him in front of her as Eibon's opened fire, his rifle chattering and spraying a stream of automatic rounds towards her. Paul's body jerked about as the bullets ripped into him. Fran tossed his corpse at Eibon. Cursing, Eibon flung himself sideways to dodge it.

"Kill that thing!" Kaliner shouted, opening up with his own rifle, firing from his hip. His bullets dug into the corridor wall as Fran ducked beneath them, racing towards him on all fours.

Tim tried to get a shot at her, but she was past Kaliner and on him before he could. She shot upwards to her feet, the claws of both her hands sinking into his groin as she lifted him from the floor, knocking him from his feet as she tore away his genitals in the process.

Kaliner had no idea why she had gone after Tim instead of him. He swung his rifle towards Fran and fired another burst at her. This time, he hit her. The three-round burst caught the young woman in her chest. Black blood oozed from the holes they tore in her. She staggered but didn't fall. Kaliner let loose again, this time on full auto but Fran jumped upwards into the shaft she had emerged from. Kaliner heard her scurrying away inside it. He hosed the ceiling, emptying his rifle's magazine in the hopes of hitting her with a lucky round.

"Oh crap!" he heard Eibon shout as he came running by where Kaliner stood.

Kaliner looked along the corridor to see what Eibon was running from to see Chris on the floor at Dillon's feet. Dillon wasn't Dillon anymore. He was covered in Chris's blood and clutched one of Chris's arms that he must have torn from him, holding it like a chicken leg. Dillon's teeth worked furiously at rending the flesh from it. Kaliner heard a new noise behind him and turned to see Tim getting to his feet. Tim's eyes were glowing a bright shade of yellow, and if he felt any pain from the mess that was his crotch, he didn't show it. Tim growled at him, showing teeth that were no longer human then sprang towards him.

The sound of automatic fire thundered again as Eibon blew Tim's head into little more than black ooze-covered pus.

"You owe me one, Sarge!" Eibon shouted at him.

Kaliner had no time to focus on anything but Dillon though. Dillon had dropped Chris's severed arm and was moving in his direction. Dillon's eyes were gone. His sockets were nothing more than areas of claw-ripped, shredded meat. Kaliner knew Dillon couldn't see him, but that didn't mean he couldn't hear and smell him.

Ejecting the spent magazine from his rifle, Kaliner slammed a fresh one into it as Dillon drew nearer to him. Kaliner readied his rifle and fired into Michael at point-blank range. The bullets he fired gutted Dillon. Strands of Dillon's intestines spilled to drop to the floor around his ankles. Kaliner didn't give Michael a chance to recover. He had seen how strong and fast whatever it was that Dillon and the others had become were. Stepping forward, Kaliner dealt Dillon a blow to the side of his skull with the butt of his rifle. It knocked Dillon over. Kaliner pressed the barrel of his rifle to Dillon's forehead and held the weapon's trigger tight.

"Yeesh, Sarge," Eibon said, stepping up beside him. "He's dead already, man."

Kaliner released his rifle's trigger and once again, ejected its magazine to slide another fresh one into it.

"Put some rounds in Chris, Paul, and Dillon's skulls too," he ordered Eibon. "I don't want either of them getting up."

"Yes, sir," Eibon croaked weakly but carried out his order. When he was done, Eibon leaned over and vomited onto the corridor floor.

"I'd say it's time we got the hell off Deck 3," Kaliner said.

"But what about Michael and Chapman?" Eibon asked, getting himself together and wiping the traces of vomit staining his lips away with his sleeve.

"You think they're alive?" Kaliner shouted and then pointed at Dillon's corpse. "Odds are, they're either dead or they've become whatever the hell those things are!"

"Right then," Eibon said. "Getting the hell out of here it is then."

Kaliner took the lead as the two of them ran full out towards the closest lift. Deck 3 had been locked down, but Kaliner had the code to override the lift lockout, and he intended to use it.

****

Captain Hall had returned to the bridge, his armed escort with him. The two soldiers took up positions at the bridge's lift doors as Hall headed for his command chair. Grey was waiting on him.

"I take it your visit to medical didn't go well?" Grey asked as Hall sat down.

Captain Hall shook his head. "We've got a virus on our hands, Grey."

"Am I to assume it came aboard with our guest from the *Homestead*, sir?"

Nodding, Hall sighed. "I don't suppose you have any good news?"

"As a matter of fact…" Grey grinned. "I do."

Grey motioned at the sensor tech. The forward screen came on containing an image of the *Pickman*. She was shot to Hell, but she was still holding together somehow.

"The *Pickman*!" Hall shouted, leaping from his seat. "When did she blink in?"

"About five minutes ago, sir," Grey told him. "We've already established contact with acting Captain Allen."

"Harrison?" Hall asked, knowing he didn't want to hear the answer.

"Dead, sir," Grey reported, "along with the majority of the *Pickman*'s crew. According to Captain Allen, there are less than forty people left alive onboard her."

"Still," Captain Hall allowed himself a smile, "she's here. We're not alone anymore, Grey."

"Indeed, we are not, sir." Grey returned his smile. It quickly faded though as Grey took on a professional tone again. "Captain Allen is requesting that he and his crew come abroad for the duration of the repairs to the *Pickman*, sir. He says they don't have the manpower or parts to repair her on their own and that she has suffered extremely dangerous damage to her structural integrity."

"Have you informed them of our own situation?" Hall asked.

"No, sir," Grey answered. "I didn't want to overstep my authority."

Hall laughed. "Good call, Grey, but we're going to have to tell Captain Allen. We can't risk him and his crew coming over here until we know more about this virus and get the mess we have on our hands under control."

"Agreed, sir." Grey nodded. "Shall I open a channel to the *Pickman*? Captain Allen has been waiting on your arrival so that he could speak with you personally."

"Do it," Hall ordered.

The image of the *Pickman* on the forward screen was replaced by one of Allen. As close in as the shot was, Hall could still see the level of destruction that had ravaged the *Pickman*'s bridge behind him. The ceiling of the *Pickman*'s bridge looked to have collapsed and the flashes of sparking wires lit the near darkness surrounding Allen.

"Captain Hall, thank God, it's good to see you!" Allen's voice was thick with hope and excitement.

"Good see you too, Allen." Hall leaned forward in his command chair. "I am sorry to hear about Harrison. He'll be sorely missed."

"He went just like he wanted to, sir," Allen said. "Fighting the bugs until the very last."

"Allen, you're a captain too now, even if just an acting one. You don't have to call me, sir," Hall chuckled.

"We've been hurt pretty bad over here, Gerald. We're going to need a lot of help if we're going to save this ship."

"I can see that," Hall nodded. "What happened over there?"

"The hit that really got us was a missile we took near our engineering section. It gutted us, leaked most of our atmosphere, and damaged our blink drive. Took us three blinks to get here."

"That explains why you're late," Hall teased.

"And no other ships made it out of Yogotha?" Allen asked.

"We're it so far," Hall told him. "I'm not expecting any more. Frag, Allen, I thought the *Pickman* was lost too."

"I don't blame you." Allen turned to bark an order at someone before returning his attention to Hall. "Yogotha was a blood bath. It's nigh a miracle any of us made it out."

Hall found he didn't have the words to respond to that statement.

"Look, Gerald, how soon can we come aboard? We've lost most of the atmosphere and this ship is barely holding together."

"About that," Hall said. "Allen, I can't let you come aboard right now. We've got our own situation we're dealing with. We took in a shuttle from the *Homestead* moments before we blinked out of Yogotha. It seems it was carrying Dr. Spinner's virus and it's gotten loose over here."

Allen appeared to gather his thoughts before he spoke again. "I thought Spinner's virus was only supposed to work on the bugs."

"We believe it's mutated somehow. We've lost several crewmen to it within the last few hours." Hall kept the fact that those deaths were the results of the efforts of a single, infected woman to himself.

"I understand your caution, Gerald, but we can't stay over here too much longer," Allen argued. "The shields holding the *Pickman* together could go anytime."

Hall thought over what to do. "I can send you whatever parts you need if we have them, Allen, but you'll have to put them through DECON before you can take them onboard. That's the best we can do at this point."

"Understood," Allen answered glumly. "We'll take what we can get."

Hall glanced over at Grey as Allen ended the transmission. Grey was frowning at whatever he was reading on the screen of the pad he held.

"What now?" Hall asked.

"Sergeant Kaliner is requesting your presence at the DECON station we sat up at the lift on Deck 4. It seems the infected young woman we have running loose has struck again."

"Great." Hall shook his head in frustration.

"Dr. Niles wants to see you as well, sir. He says he has a more complete report on Spinner's virus and what it has become."

"Tell Dr. Niles I'll be there as soon as I can." Hall got out of his command chair. "Something tells me I need to pay a visit to Sergeant Kaliner first though."

****

Dr. Niles sat at his desk in his office, which was a closed-off section of Med-Bay 1, reading through the test results on Marshall's blood again. He'd had read them twice already. Spinner's work was nothing short of genius. Even mutated into something without an airborne vector, it was infectious as hades. It did appear to be spread by the teeth and nails of its hosts. The slightest scratch from an infected person was enough to spread it. After that initial infection, it worked rapidly to alter its host on a D.N.A. level, changing them into something no longer human.

The virus gave its host increased speed, strength, and stamina on a level unlike anything Dr. Niles had ever seen before. As impressive as those things were, it was the virus's regenerative properties that left Dr. Niles in awe. If the data he was reading was correct, it was possible that a host of the virus might be able even grow lost limbs like certain types of reptiles, only at such a rapid rate that it seemed impossible. The data didn't lie though. Spinner's virus was a work of art. Apparently, it had been designed to turn one bug against another while giving the infected bug the edge. That explained why the young woman from the *Homestead* had turned feral upon the virus taking hold within her.

The medic, Marshall, was surely infected too from the wound she had dealt him. Dr. Niles had ordered Marshall sedated with triple the normal dose of sedatives. He had also ordered Nurse Rachel to restrain Marshall. Dr. Niles wasn't taking any chances with something as dangerous as the virus was proving to be. He wanted Marshall alive though so that he could study the active virus in his blood. It was almost a certainty that the virus had no cure. Spinner would have seen to that. However, Spinner, as gifted as he was, was still just a man. Dr. Niles hoped that with further study he could at least create a vaccine against the virus.

Dr. Niles got up from his desk and moved to the sealed containment case that held the case the infected young lieutenant had brought aboard with her. It was likely that inside the case Spinner had sent along his notes on his work and the virus. Dr. Niles had been hesitant about attempting to open the case, but now, so much could depend on the data that might be inside it.

He was in the process beginning to work towards that goal when he heard Nurse Rachel cry out from the depths of Med-Bay

1. Dr. Niles rushed out of his office, his heart pounding within his chest and adrenaline surging through his veins.

Dr. Niles skidded to a stop as he entered the patient area of Med-Bay 1. The infected medic, Marshall, had broken free of his restraints and apparently shrugged off the triple dose of sedatives he had been given. Marshall's eyes glowed yellow. They were full of a feral hunger that sent chills through Dr. Niles. Nurse Rachel was dead. Her corpse lay on the Med-Bay's floor at Marshall's feet. Marshall looked to have snapped her neck.

Marshall cocked his head sideways staring at him as Dr. Niles began to back up slowly.

Dr. Niles spotted a scalpel on a nearby tray of medical instruments and snatched it up, holding it like a knife as Marshall advanced towards him at an unhurried pace.

"Stay back!" Dr. Niles shouted at the infected medic.

In response, Marshall snarled, showing the jagged, razor-like teeth that filled his mouth.

Dr. Niles didn't dare turn to make a run for it. He knew Marshall, infected by the virus, would be much faster than he could ever hope to be. No, his only chance was to stand and fight. The scalpel was a poor weapon, but it was all he had.

As Marshall sprang at him, Dr. Niles lashed out with the scalpel. Its blade sunk deep into the flesh of Marshall's neck. Black blood spurted from the wound but did nothing to slow the infected medic down. Marshall's hands closed on Dr. Niles' shoulders, pulling him forward, as he titled his head to get at Dr. Niles' throat. Dr. Niles felt the sharp points of Marshall's teeth break his skin but managed to yank away before they sunk in too deeply. He shoved against Marshall with all the strength he could muster, catching the infected medic by surprise. Marshall, caught off balance, slammed into a nearby bed, falling onto it.

Dr. Niles had lost his scalpel and was now weaponless. He turned, running towards his office, hoping to make it there and seal its door to keep Marshall out. Marshall had recovered and was on him before it had even made it halfway there. The infected medic caught him from behind, flinging him against one of the Med-Bay's walls. Dr. Niles cried out as he struck the wall, the bone of his right arm breaking, trapped between the metal of the wall and the force of his own weight. He stayed on his feet though.

As Marshall came at him again, Dr. Niles grabbed a data pad from the top of a workstation and swung it at Marshall's head. The data pad shattered at it made contact with Marshall's skull, but it did its job. Marshall staggered sideways, giving Dr. Niles a chance to sprint towards his office again. This time, he made it. He punched the controls of the office's door as soon as he was through them. The door slid shut just as Marshall reached it. Dr. Niles heard the infected medic slam into it, but it held.

Dr. Niles staggered towards his desk and collapsed into his chair there. He stared at the door listening as Marshall continued to rage against it. Raising his fingers to the wound on his throat, Dr. Niles knew he was dead. His body would live on, but as the virus that now surely pumped through his veins took hold, his mind would be lost. He would be nothing more than an instinct-driven animal. Dr. Niles could already feel the virus burning within him and knew he had very little time left.

****

"You're telling me that a lone, unarmed woman took out your entire squad except for the two of you?" Captain Hall raged.

"She wasn't human anymore, sir," Sergeant Kaliner answered.

"She tore through us like a force of nature, sir," Eibon added.

"Did I ask you?" Captain Hall snapped at Eibon.

Eibon lowered his gaze towards the floor. "No, sir, you didn't."

"She wasn't exactly alone either, sir," Kaliner added.

"What does that mean?" Captain Hall leaned over to slam his palms down onto the top of the table that the two soldiers sat at.

"My men, sir, I mean the ones she hurt, they changed too," Kaliner said. "They got up and came after us too."

Captain Hall backed up from the table, looking at the two soldiers. He struggled to control the anger he was feeling before he spoke again. "So how many infected are we dealing with now?"

"Just the woman captain," Kaliner told him. "We were able to stop the others."

"And how did you do that?" Captain Hall demanded.

"Even ramped up like they are strength wise, sir, those things are still human enough to die," Eibon spoke up. "We put bullets in their skulls and they stopped moving pretty quickly."

"I see," Captain Hall sighed. "Sergeant Kaliner, would you advise sending in more men to eliminate your original target?"

"Not if there's any other option, Captain," Kaliner said. "If we send in more men, we run the risk of her turning them too. She's damn fast, sir. Smart too. If she's able to get the drop on you, you're dead, no question."

"Deck 3 is fully locked down," Captain Hall reminded the two soldiers. "Do you think that will be enough to keep her there?"

"Hard to say, sir," Kaliner admitted. "Like I said, she's smart. She might be able to find a way out that a sane, normal person would never consider trying."

"Then what do you suggest we do?" Captain Hall pressed.

"I don't know, sir," Kaliner shrugged. "Deck 3 is sealed off. Maybe we could cut its oxygen."

Captain Hall was truly impressed by the suggestion and wondered why he hadn't thought of doing it himself. "That could work," he nodded.

Suddenly, the room's light went out, plunging it into utter darkness. He heard the two soldiers leaping up from their seats and the sound of them drawing their pistols. As spooked as Kaliner and Eibon were, Captain Hall hoped they didn't shoot him before the lights came back on, assuming they did.

"Stand down!" he barked at them. "We're alone in here!"

At that moment, the lights did come back on. It wasn't the normal lights of the room though. It was the dim, red glow of the *Magnum*'s emergency lighting.

The comm. Captain Hall wore on his wrist chimed.

"Captain," his XO, Grey, called out over the comm. "I need you to get the bridge at once, sir."

"What's going on?" Captain Hall demanded.

There was a brief pause before Grey answered him. "The virus, sir, it's spread. We've lost all contact with engineering and the hangar bay where the shuttle from the *Homestead* came aboard."

"God have mercy on us," Captain Hall muttered. He looked at the two soldiers that shared the room with him. "You two, you're with me."

"Yes, sir!" Sergeant Kaliner and Eibon chorused together.

The two soldiers' gear rested on the floor beneath the table they had been sitting at. They began to get suited up for combat again.

Captain Hall extended his hand towards them. "Sergeant, I'm going to need you to surrender your sidearm."

Kaliner handed it to him.

"You know how to use that, sir?" Kaliner asked him.

Captain Hall checked the weapon to make sure it was loaded and ready for use. He laughed and said, "I wasn't always a ship captain, Sergeant."

"I can see that sir." Kaliner grinned at him.

Turning to the door leading out of the room, Captain Hall paused. "We have no idea what we're about to walk into out there. We need to reach the bridge though, at all costs."

The two soldiers nodded.

"If we run into anyone who appears to be infected, don't let them touch you. Dr. Niles believes this virus is spread through the wounds the infected inflict on their victims."

"That fits with what we saw on Deck 3, sir," Sergeant Kaliner agreed as he moved between Captain Hall and the door. "I'll be taking point, sir; that is, if you don't mind."

"Not at all, Sergeant Kaliner," Captain Hall assured him. "You're the professional at this. I'll be right behind you."

Kaliner opened the door looking as if he half expected to see one of the infected come flying through it at them. He looked along both sides of the corridor, making sure it was clear, before stepping out into it. Captain Hall followed after him with Eibon bringing up the rear.

****

Grey paced about the *Magnum*'s bridge. He felt utterly helpless, and in truth, there was little he could do about the infection that appeared to be spreading like wildfire across the ship. He'd been in tough spots before but never anything like this. He almost wished he was back in the Yogotha system with Swarm missiles streaking towards the *Magnum*. At least then, he would know how to respond to the threat he was up against.

Two, heavily armed soldiers stood next to the bridge's lift doors. Grey was thankful they were there. The sight of the rifles in their hands brought him some comfort. He didn't think the infected could figure out a means to get onto the bridge, given that only personnel with high enough access status had the clearance for the lift's A.I. to bring them to it, but he knew that both he and Captain Hall had badly underestimated what the infected were capable of since the existence of the virus aboard the *Magnum* had been discovered.

The creepy, dim glow of the ship's emergency lights didn't do anything to help his nerves. The situation aboard the *Pickman* was growing worse as well. Grey had overseen several, carefully coordinated shipment of parts that were desperately needed for the ship's repair efforts but even so, there were so few crewmen left alive over there with the skills needed to get them installed and functional that Grey knew the parts alone weren't going to be enough to save the *Pickman*. If the *Magnum* was unable to send technical help soon, the *Pickman* would die just as surely as she would have if she hadn't escaped the Yogotha system.

Captain Allen had made several calls pressing him for that help, but Grey couldn't provide it. The risk of the virus loose on the *Magnum* was too high to even consider doing so. It was hard on Grey to refuse the help Allen was begging for, but his hands were tied. Everything had gone south so quickly. Less than a day had passed since the virus had been brought aboard the *Magnum*, and already they were fighting for their lives.

Grey wished Captain Hall would hurry up. Perhaps he could find an answer to it all. Reports continued to pour in of the virus spreading. The *Magnum* was at General Quarters and Deck 3 was locked down, but neither had seemed to even slow the spread of the virus, much less stop it.

****

Sergeant Kaliner came to an abrupt halt ahead of Captain Hall and Eibon, raising his hand to tell them to stop as well.

The corridors of the *Magnum* reminded Captain Hall of the warzones he had dropped into during his early days in the Republic military before he had transferred into the Navy. Every time they came across the body of a dead crewman, the three of them would stop long enough for Kaliner to make sure that crewman wasn't going to be getting up to come after them. It was grisly work. They didn't have a lot of ammo with them, and even if they had, Kaliner likely wouldn't have risked using a firearm for fear of the sound of it being fired drawing the infected to their position.

Kaliner and Eibon carried combat knives in their gear and it was those they used on the bodies. The two of them took turns as to who had to deal with the bodies. Whenever they came across one, one of the two soldiers would squat down beside it to ram the blade of their knife into its skull and destroy its brain. There appeared to be no other sure means of making sure the infected wouldn't get to its fight again.

In the distance, Captain Hall could hear a woman screaming. Every instinct in him urged him to run to help her. Only Kaliner's grim expression held him back. Kaliner was on point and could see around the bend in the corridor where he couldn't.

"There are two of the infected, sir," Kaliner informed him. "They're...eating her alive."

Captain Hall bit his lip but said nothing.

"No way around them I'm afraid," Kaliner told him. "We're going to have to go through them if we want to make it to the lift."

Captain Hall nodded, checking the pistol in his hand yet again to make sure it was ready when the time came.

"I got movement behind us," Eibon called out.

"Infected?" Kaliner asked.

"Can't tell yet," Eibon answered. "I can just hear them coming."

"We don't want to get caught between two groups of those monsters," Captain Hall said.

"No argument there, sir," Kaliner shrugged, "but it may not be up to us."

"Forward then," Captain Hall ordered.

"Forward it is." Kaliner frowned.

The sergeant sprang around the corner of the corridor, his rifle blazing away on full auto. Captain Hall followed him as Eibon hung back.

Captain Hall saw the two infected as he came around the corner. One was a man, his uniform drenched in the blood of the woman he was holding to the floor of the corridor. She struggled against his grip on her shoulders, legs kicking wildly, as the other infected leaned over her, its face pressed against her mid-section. The other infected, whose teeth ripped and tore at the woman's stomach, lifted her head at the sound of Kaliner's rifle. Kaliner's first three-round burst struck the infected male, knocking it away from the woman it had been holding down. Black pus leaked from the wounds the bullets ripped in its chest. The female infected sprang to her feet, bounding towards the sergeant.

Captain Hall jerked up his pistol and put a carefully aimed round into her skull. The infected woman flopped backwards to land on the floor, a ragged hole in the center of her forehead. She didn't get up.

The male infected though was far from done. He came at Kaliner with rage burning in his yellow eyes. Kaliner barely had time to fire another burst. Kaliner aimed at the infected's head, but it was moving too fast. One of the rounds missed entirely. Another blew a chunk out of the infected's right shoulder, sending black pus-like blood splashing across the corridor. The last round tore into the infected's throat, blowing a gaping hole in its center. The infected stumbled, giving Kaliner time to finish it. All three of the rounds he fired this time struck the infected's skull. It exploded in a mess of flying bone fragments and brain matter. The infected male's body collapsed to land beside the woman it had been attacking when they arrived. She screamed, trying to roll away from it, but the woman could barely move. Her gut was open from just above her pelvis to the bottom of her ribs. Captain Hall could see the purple, red-slicked strands of her intestines sliding around inside her as she tried to move.

Captain Hall started to move to help her, but Kaliner stopped him, grabbing him by the shoulder.

"You know she's dead, sir," Kaliner told him. "Nothing we can do but finish it."

Before Captain Hall could protest, the sergeant aimed at the whimpering woman's face and blew it apart with a quick, three-round burst from his rifle.

Eibon raced around the corner of the corridor to join them, his face so pale it was as white as freshly fallen snow.

"We got company!" Eibon shouted as he took up a firing position facing the way he had come from.

Sergeant Kaliner and Captain Hall turned as well just as a trio of the infected came charging at them. Kaliner and Eibon's rifles chattered as they fired into the infected. The first of the infected was caught by their combined streams of fire. Their bullets shredded its chest into something resembling ground meat. It went toppling back into the path of the other two infected behind it. They dodged its falling body, one going to the right, the other cutting to the left, their fierce pace unchanged.

Eibon swept his rifle around to target the left one as Kaliner took aim at the other. The one Eibon targeted took a burst that blew its left arm from its shoulder, but it kept right on coming. Kaliner went for a head shot. He got lucky. Two of the three rounds of the burst he fired missed the infected woman, but the third clipped the side of her head, knocking her off balance and causing her to stagger. Kaliner fired again and the woman's head exploded in a shower of gore. Eibon's rifle clicked empty as he tried to take another shot at the approaching infected on his side of the corridor. He had no time to eject his weapon's magazine and reload it. Spinning his rifle around in his grasp, he brought its butt up to use it like a club. He never got the chance to though.

Captain Hall stepped forward as his pistol rang out. A hole blossomed between the eyes of the infected racing at Eibon.

"Thanks." Eibon nodded at him, already at work on reloading his rifle.

"There are more of them coming!" Kaliner yelled as he tore a grenade from his belt and activated it.

Captain Hall stared at him with wide eyes. Was the man insane? This was a corridor inside a battleship, not an open battlefield. "Stop!" Captain Hall ordered, but it was too late. Kaliner had already lobbed the grenade around the bend in the corridor and was running towards him.

"Get down!" Kaliner shouted at Eibon as he plowed into Captain Hall, taking him to the floor beneath him.

The explosion shook the corridor.

"You idiot!" Captain Hall screamed as Sergeant Kaliner yanked him back to his feet.

"Come on, sir!" Kaliner urged him. "A blast that size is for sure going to have any other of those things on this deck coming out the woodwork at us."

The three men sprinted along the corridor, racing for the lift that would take them to the bridge. The lift doors opened as they approached, spilling four infected who were trapped inside it into the corridor. Snarling, they launched themselves at the three men. Kaliner, who was in the lead, tried to bring up his rifle to block the infected crewman springing at him. He was only partially successful. The rifle, turned sideways, body-checked the infected, but its claws raked Kaliner's arms, digging deep into his flesh. Kaliner shoved the infected back, knocking it into one of the others behind it.

Eibon's rifle chattered as he sent two of the infected sprawling, riddled with bullets. Captain Hall did his best to get into a firing position to target the two infected that were engaged with Kaliner but failed. Kaliner had swung his rifle about in his hands to use as a club, smashing it into the face of one of the infected. The rifle broke apart from the force of the blow as it shattered the jaw of the infected woman Kaliner had struck. The other infected crewman had come at Kaliner again though, and this time, succeeded in reaching him. The infected crewman tackled Kaliner, taking them both to the floor of the corridor. Kaliner was able to twist about and place his self on top of the infected crewman. The sergeant grabbed his boot knife, sliding it free of its sheath. Its blade gleamed in the dim red lights of the corridor as Kaliner rammed it into the infected crewman's mouth. The blade broke teeth as it entered. Kaliner put his weight onto the knife, driving it through the back of the infected crewman's throat. Black blood erupted from the infected's mouth, running over Kaliner's hands.

As the female infected came at Kaliner, her broken jaw dangling and dripping blood, Captain Hall finally got a shot at her. His pistol barked as fired one round after another into her chest. Each bullet tore a gaping hole in her flesh. His shots knocked her away from Sergeant Kaliner like he had intended. Captain Hall heard Eibon's rifle thunder as the soldier finished her with a three-round burst to the side of her head that sent black blood and brain matter spraying outward with the bullets as they exited the other side of her skull.

Captain Hall looked at Sergeant Kaliner where he sat on top of the infected he had taken out with his knife. The sergeant's expression was grim as he met Captain Hall's eyes.

"I'm dead, sir," Kaliner told him. "It's just a matter of time. You know what you have to do."

Eibon was silent, watching the interaction between the two of them.

"You're right, Sergeant," Captain Hall said. "I'm sorry."

Captain Hall walked over to Kaliner, pressing the barrel of his pistol against the sergeant's forehead.

"It's been an honor..." Kaliner started, but Captain Hall squeezed the pistol's trigger before the sergeant was able to finish.

The shot echoed in the confined space of the corridor as Kaliner's body toppled sideways to rest on the floor in front of Captain Hall.

"That was cold, man," Eibon said.

"Had to be done," Captain Hall told him.

The sound of more infected approaching them at a frantic pace could be heard from further down the corridor.

"Time to go, sir," Eibon said, already racing into the lift ahead of him.

Captain Hall took one final, sad look at Kaliner's sprawled-out corpse then followed after him.

****

When the virus had broken loose in the hangar bay and things had gone to hell, Brent had taken shelter inside one of the shuttles docked there. He still held the large wrench he had used to bash in Anna's brains in his hands. The smell of vomit inside the shuttle was intense. He had vomited up everything his body could heave out after killing her. He hadn't had a choice though. After her eyes had turned yellow, she'd torn through her own deck crew like some kind of rampaging monster. Brent had watched Anna kill two men and wound several others before he had finally found the courage to stop her. All it had taken was a single blow to her skull from behind with the wrench he had been working with. The strength he had put into the blow had folded the top of her head inward with the sickening sound of cracking bone.

Brent had worked with Anna for a long time and knew her well. It had nearly ripped out his heart to do what he had to do. Stopping Anna though was only the start. There were other members of the deck crew that had turned when she did. Brent didn't know what had caused his friends to turn into monsters and knew he couldn't fight them all. He had high-tailed it to the closest shuttle and locked himself inside it. Brent had imagined his friends who had turned would come after him, pounding on the shuttle's doors or trying to smash through its forward window, but they hadn't. Instead, they had gone after all the members of the deck crew who were still human. Brent had watched them all be run down and torn apart. When everyone in the hangar had either turned or was dead, the monsters had left the hangar in search of more prey.

An hour had passed since he had seen any of the yellow-eyed freaks outside the shuttle in the hangar. During that time, he had reported into the bridge to let them know what had happened in the hangar. The ship's XO, Grey, had taken his call personally and advised him to remain where he was. Grey had explained that a virus had been brought aboard the *Magnum* by the shuttle from the *Homestead* and that the entire crew was now fighting for their lives against it. Brent didn't understand all of what Grey told him, but he knew he was sick of sitting in the shuttle and smelling his own vomit.

Brent felt like a coward for not doing more to help save those he could before taking shelter in the shuttle and desperately wanted to exit the shuttle and see what he could do to help the rest of the ship. His fear and the memory of killing Anna kept him inside it though. Brent had considered powering up the shuttle and making a run for the *Pickman*. He had heard about the *Pickman*'s arrival before everything had gone south in the hangar. Grey had given him a direct order to remain where he was and wait for help, but something inside of Brent told him that help was never going to come and that he was on his own.

The shuttle was fully equipped with gear and emergency kits. Brent made his way to where they were stored in the shuttle's rear and started going through them. He ignored the combat armor he found there, knowing it would only slow him down. It wasn't meant to stop claws and teeth and would leave good portions of his body exposed even if he suited up in a set of it.

What he did take though was two of the rifles he found. He made sure both were loaded and ready for action. He slung one onto his shoulder by its strap and held the other in by its grip in his right hand as he made up his mind to leave the shuttle and venture into the corridors of the *Magnum.*

He disengaged the lock of the shuttle's side door and slid it open. The hangar was quiet, and there was still no sign of any of the infected. Brent stepped out of the shuttle and headed for the closest exit from the hangar.

The partially eaten corpses of several of his friends and co-workers littered the hangar's floor. Brent gave them a wide berth as he made his way across the hangar towards the exit. They all looked to be truly dead, but Grey had warned him that the infected were extremely tough to kill and to exercise caution when dealing with them. Destroying an infected person's brain was the only means of being sure that they wouldn't get back up according to Grey.

Brent heard a loud clatter to his right as a toolkit was knocked from the top of a worktable, spilling its contents on the metal floor of the hangar. His head jerked around in the direction the noise had come from. He saw a woman with blazing yellow eyes standing next to the worktable. She made no move towards him. She just stared at him as her lips twitched, showing him glimpses of the jagged teeth inside her mouth. His brain told him he knew the woman from somewhere as they continued to stare at each other. Then suddenly he realized she was the woman from the shuttle that had come in from the *Homestead.* Her name was Lieutenant Fran or something like that.

"I don't want any trouble," Brent's heavy voice rumbled.

The woman's lips stopped twitching as they parted reshaping themselves into a feral snarl that reminded Brent that whoever she had been was gone now, and only the monster she had become existed now. Her veins were swollen and pulsed beneath her skin. She reared her head and gave an inhuman shriek that sent Brent staggering backwards in utter terror. By the time he remembered he was holding a rifle in his hands, she was running towards him. Brent fired the rifle. Spent shell casings flew from its side to clatter to the floor at his feet as he held the weapon's trigger tight. The woman anticipated and jumped into the air, avoiding the barrage of fire he threw at her. Her claws dug into the metal of the hangar's ceiling, and she scrambled across it like some sort of deranged-looking insect.

Brent jerked his rifle upwards and spun around as she skittered over him, but by the time he had, the woman had vanished from his sight. His gaze darted this way and that, scanning the hangar for any sign of the infected woman. He never saw her atop the shuttle docked to his left until she leaped from its roof at him. She slammed into him, sending his rifle flying from his grasp. Brent barely managed to grab her wrists in his hands to keep her claws from slashing out his eyes.

The two of them wrestled. Brent's thick muscles bulged from the strain of keeping his hold on the woman's wrists. Her strength was incredible. Her head snapped forward as she went after him with her teeth. Brent hadn't been expecting the move. Her teeth ripped a good size chunk of meat from his right arm. Screaming from the pain and the sight of his own blood spurting from the wound, the infected woman had inflicted, Brent released his grip on her wrists, staggering away from her. The woman continued her attack. The claws of both her hands swiped at Brent, slashing deep, long grooves in the shoulder he turned towards her.

Brent stumbled but wasn't out of the fight. He spun around, smashing a fist into her face. Her nose crunched beneath the force of the blow. Brent followed up with a blow to her stomach and was rewarded by the sound of her breath being knocked from her lungs. The woman slumped to the floor in front of him. Brent pressed his advantage, lashing out with a kick that flipped her over onto her back.

The woman snatched Brent's leg, her nails digging into him, and yanked the big man from his feet. Brent crashed onto the floor with a loud thud. His eyes were wide with fear as the woman jumped on top of him. The thumb of her right hand plunged into his left eye, pushing it from its socket. It dangled against his cheek, still attached by a thin strand of sinew. Brent thrashed about, trying to fling the woman away as she ground her thumb around inside the socket his left eye had occupied. Blood flowed like tears from the socket she continued to ravage. Brent reached up to grab at her but was too slow. The fingers of her other hands wound themselves into his hair, getting a firm hold on it. With that hand, she rammed Brent's head into the metal floor, over and over, in a savage rage.

Brent was blinded by pain in the moments before his world went black.

****

Fran sat atop the big man's chest, her legs spread over it. The fight was over. He was hers to do with whatever she wanted. Removing the thumb of her right hand from the big man's eye socket, she raised it to her lips. Her long, pointed tongue emerged from her mouth to lick at the blood covering her thumb. She considered reaching into the big man's chest and tearing his rib cage apart to taste his innards but didn't. She was learning to control her hunger just enough to resist the urge to do so. Instead, she took hold of the big man's jaws, forcing his mouth open.

Leaning closer to the big man's face, Fran opened her mouth. Her body heaved as her back arched like a cat coughing up a hairball. A thick glob of blackish ooze worked its way up her throat and dropped from her mouth into that of the big man's. It splattered over his face, but the bulk of it found its way into his open mouth. The big man's body began to spasm beneath her.

Fran removed herself from the man's chest, getting to her feet. She watched the big man's body writhe about on the floor. His spasming form hit a crescendo of pitching about then stopped moving as he died and was born again.

Brent's remaining eye fluttered open. A yellow glow shined out from within it. With an animal like growl that rumbled up his throat, Brent sprang to his feet.

Fran cocked her head sideways as she appraised the newest of her children. He was indeed a beautiful sight, so strong, so hungry. She issued a series of bark-like grunts, commanding him to follow her as she raced towards the hangar's exit. His heavy footfalls sounded like thunder as he ran after her.

She could sense that most of the ship's crew now belonged to her and they, too, were hungry. It was time to finish her work. She didn't understand how she knew, but Fran knew that the last of those left alive would be found on the ship's bridge. All she had to do was gather her children and lead them there.

****

The two armed guards spun towards the lift as its doors opened onto the bridge.

"Hold your fire!" Captain Hall shouted at them as he saw the barrels of their rifles aimed at himself and Eibon.

The guards immediately recognized who he was and lowered their weapons.

"Thank God!" Captain Hall heard his XO, Grey, shout.

Grey rushed forward to meet him as Captain Hall stepped out of the lift onto the bridge.

"Report!" Captain Hall snapped at Grey.

"We've lost the ship, sir," Grey told him. "As far as we can tell, this bridge is the last area that's still secure against the infected."

"God helped us," Captain Hall rasped. He'd expected things to be bad but...

"How?" Captain Hall asked.

"From what I can piece together, the hangar crew that rescued Lieutenant Fran from the wreckage of the crashed shuttle from the *Homestead,* well, some of them were infected by the virus somehow. When they turned, they attacked the others in the bay, turning them as well. From there, they spread out to engineering and then rest of the ship." Grey paused. "We did everything we could to stop them, sir, but..."

"I saw what was happening out there, Grey," Captain Hall assured him. "No one could have stopped it from happening with the entire hangar crew pouring into the ship's corridors."

"Thank you, sir," Grey said, looking relieved.

"Captain..." one of the two armed guards hesitantly said.

Captain Hall glared at the guard but couldn't fault him for doing his job. "You need to check us out, make sure we're not infected?"

"Yes, sir." The guard frowned.

"Let's get it over with then," Captain Hall ordered.

The two guards checked him and Eibon over for claw and bite marks. Finding none, they backed away from Captain Hall and Eibon to take up their positions at the lift door again.

"Now," Captain Hall said as he walked over to his command chair and plopped into it. "It's time we figure out how we're going to get through this alive shall we?"

Grey nodded eagerly. "The *Pickman* is still holding on, sir. I think Captain Allen has finally given up on convincing us to allow its survivors to board the *Magnum*. It appears he's beginning to realize just how bad things have become over here."

"And what is the status of the *Pickman*?" Captain Hall asked.

"We were able to deliver two shuttle loads of parts to it before we lost the hangar. Captain Allen reports that they have stabilized the *Pickman*'s life-support systems. And his people have continued to do what they can to bring its primary systems on-line again."

"What about the Swarm?" Captain Hall gestured at the stars on the forward view screen.

"No sign of any bug warships, sir," Grey assured him. "It's very possible that we've lost them entirely. This system we blinked into is well beyond our own star charts, likely theirs as well."

"Well, that at least is good news," Captain Hall grunted.

"Sort of ironic isn't it, sir?" Grey chuckled darkly.

"What's that?" Captain Hall stared at his XO.

"We finally escape the bugs, sir, only to be taken out by a virus we created to wipe them out," Grey said.

"We're not dead yet, Grey," Captain Hall reminded him. "As long as we're alive, there's hope."

"Of course, Captain," Grey agreed, though he didn't really sound like he believed the words he said.

"Does Captain Allen believe he'll be able to restore the *Pickman*'s blink drive?"

"Not without more help and parts, sir," Grey said. "And even then, it's unlikely that the *Pickman* will hold together for more than a few blinks with all the damage to her overall structure and hull."

"Taking our chances on the *Pickman* might be wiser than trying to remain here," Captain Hall pointed out. He glanced around the bridge. Counting himself, Eibon, and the two guards, those on the bridge totaled eleven remaining uninfected human beings. "If the eleven of us are really all that's left onboard this ship…"

"I know what you're thinking, sir, but even if all of us ourselves in quarantine upon our arrival over there, there's still no certainty that we wouldn't just be carrying the virus over there with us," Grey argued.

Captain Hall shrugged, "You have a better plan then?"

"No, sir," Grey shook his head.

"Then I don't think we have any choice but take that chance if any of us want to live through this madness."

"There's also the issue of reaching the hangar bay, sir," Grey told him. "We'd have to fight our way through the entire army of infected that are out there in the corridors, sir."

"I'd rather go out fighting than just sitting here waiting to die," Eibon spoke up.

Grey shot him a *who in the devil are you* look.

"That's Eibon," Captain Hall told Grey. "Without him, I'd be dead or one of those things myself. I trust his judgment, Grey. So what do you think, Eibon? Could we make it to the hangar bay?"

"It would be rough, Captain, and we'd certainly lose folks along the way," Eibon said honestly after a moment of thinking over the question.

"But you truly believe we would have a chance of at least some of us making it?" Captain Hall pressed.

Eibon nodded. "I think so, sir, a chance at least."

"We'd need to take whatever parts Captain Allen still needs with us in order to repair the *Pickman* or we would just be trading one tomb for another, sir," Grey said.

"Good point," Captain Hall agreed. "Get on the comm. and find out what those last parts are Grey. In the meantime, Eibon, I want you to work up a plan for all us to make a run for the hangar."

"Yes, sir!" the two of them answered him in chorus.

Captain Hall slumped deeper into his chair as they went about carrying out his orders. He rested his head in his hands and closed his eyes. His body was already pushed to its limits and the exhaustion was catching up with him. He figured this was as much rest as he was going to get before all of them plunged into the hell of the *Magnum*'s corridors to fight tooth and nail for their very lives.

****

Fran led her army of children to the doors of a lift on Deck 4. They snarled and filled the corridor behind her. The big one she had turned in the hangar bay kept close to her side. She enjoyed his presence and his smell. He was, in a sense, an extension of herself even more so than the rest of those she had turned.

The lift was the key to reaching the bridge and the last of the uninfected humans aboard the ship. Oh their flesh would taste sweet upon her lips as she shredded it with her teeth and her tongue lapped up their blood.

Deep within her mind was a shadowed memory of needing to use the keypad next to the lift's door in order to get it open since it had not opened itself upon her approach. The memory of how to use it and the codes that were needed had long vanished if they had ever existed within her. She moved closer still to the lift door. The claw-like nails of her fingertips pressed against it. She raked them along the surface of the door. They tore at the paint on it but didn't pierce its metal. Something told her that she would not be able to open the door.

Stepping aside, she gestured for the big man that was now a part of her to come forward. He did, slowly. There was no need to vocalize her intent. She could reach into his mind with her own to show him her desires.

He gave a loud groan as he stepped up to the door. The claws of his fingers worked into the groove where the lift door was sealed. They dug into its metal as he got a firm grip upon the side of the lift door. With a vicious, angry roar, his thick muscles went tight beneath the tattered and blood-stained sleeves of his uniform, the swollen veins that could be seen through his skin pulsing harder.

Metal whined as the big man ripped the lift's door from it and flung it aside. It caught two of her other children, crushing them beneath its weight, but Fran didn't care. She had more than enough children for the task that lay ahead of her. They were expendable.

Fran peered into the darkness of the lift's shaft, surprised and confused not to see the lift behind the torn open door. Then she heard it in the shaft far above the deck she and her children were gathered on.

Issuing a series of commanding snarls, she ordered several of her children into the shaft. They leaped inside to begin scaling the walls of the shaft, upwards, towards the noise of the moving lift.

Soon, she thought, soon they would all feast upon the last humans and the ship would be theirs.

****

Eibon had cautioned Captain Hall against using the bridge's lift to reach the hangar so they had been forced to come up with another means of doing so. They had opted to use the *Magnum*'s maintenance shafts instead. Grey had strongly protested the idea. If they encountered the infected inside the shafts, there would be no hope of truly fighting them in such a confined space. Captain Hall had seen no other option though.

As he dropped from the shaft he had been crawling through to the floor of the hangar where Eibon and one of the soldiers from the bridge waited, Captain Hall was glad he had listened to Eibon. They had made it through the long sets of ladders and crawlspaces without encountering a single one of the infected.

Captain Hall waited for the others behind him to clear the maintenance shaft and drop into the hangar with them. He took a look around as he did so. The hangar was littered with the partially eaten bodies of the men and women who had been the hangar's crew. The smell of their rotting flesh made him gag. He covered his mouth and nose with his right hand, forcing himself to remain professional. There was no time to puke his guts out or shed tears for those that had been lost to the virus.

Eibon was already moving about the hangar bay, searching for a shuttle that would fit their needs. Two other soldiers took up defensive positions so that their angles of fire could cover all the entrances to the hangar bay.

Grey had gotten a short list of the parts that Captain Allen required in order to bring the *Pickman*'s blink drive back on-line. He and the rest of the bridge crew set about the hangar, searching for the parts on that list. Taskforce Hope protocol demanded that such parts be stored in areas where they could be easily reached and loaded onto shuttles should a ship need to be abandoned. Captain Hall had faith that they would find what they needed for the *Pickman*.

As he stood watching the others go about their efforts, Captain Hall couldn't help but wonder where the infected were. He knew they had been dispersed about the whole of the ship, and as thus, there should have been at least some of the creatures waiting on them here, but there were none. Something had pulled them away from the hangar. He was thankful for that. They lacked the firepower and numbers to fight their way through too many of the creatures, but their absence also sent up warning flags for him. Regardless, he supposed it was only a matter of time until the infected discovered where he and the others from the bridge had fled to. Sooner or later, they would show up and when they did, he could only hope that they would be ready.

Between the damage done to the hangar bay and the *Magnum*'s primary power off-line, it was impossible to close the entrances. Captain Hall counted them lucky that the shields separating the interior of the bay from the airless void outside the ship were still holding. Lowering them would be easy when the time came. All the shuttles had the comm. needed for him to log into the *Magnum*'s core systems with his command codes to shut them down.

Eibon had selected a suitable shuttle and then turned his attention to distributing weapons to those who were unarmed. Captain Hall accepted a rifle from him with a wide smile, shoving his pistol into the belt of his uniform. "Thanks."

"My pleasure, sir." Eibon grinned at him. "At least in your case, I know you're trained in how to use it. Most of your bridge crew aren't."

"Not much call for using a rifle in the Navy," Captain Hall joked.

"Reckon not, sir," Eibon agreed. "At least until you're boarded."

It felt good to laugh even if it only lasted a brief second.

Eibon cleared his throat, giving him an awkward look. "Uh, Captain, I am not sure how to ask this but…"

Captain Hall stopped him. "Let me guess. We need someone to fly the shuttle and no one else has the training."

"Exactly, sir," Eibon looked relieved.

"It's been a while since I have flown hands on instead of just barking orders from a command chair, Eibon, but I'm sure I can handle it. I'll get aboard and start the pre-flight."

"Just make sure you hurry, sir," Eibon told him. "We're pretty exposed here. When those things show up, it's going to be a bloodbath."

"Roger that, soldier." Captain Hall saluted Eibon and ran for the shuttle.

****

It was Clyde, one of the two soldiers who had been standing guard on the bridge, that saw the infected first as they began to pour into the hangar bay.

"We've got company!" he shouted. "And a lot of it too!"

Eibon took charge of the situation, despite the fact that Grey was among the crowd of survivors clustered outside of the shuttle, as he saw the infected were only coming through the entrances on the hangar's port side. If the XO had an issue with it, Grey kept it to himself, allowing Eibon to run the show.

"Hit 'em with everything you got!" he ordered. "We're either going to make it out of here or we're not. No sense in trying to conserve ammo!"

The officers from the bridge, Grey included, handled their weapons poorly, but it didn't matter. They still laid fire in the right direction. The infected were all coming through the port doors, and as thus, were packed tightly together until they got clear of them. Some had and were already starting to spread out. Eibon targeted those as the fire from the bridge officers slaughtered those making their way through the hangar doors by the dozens. The bodies of the infected began to pile up outside the two doors, but still the monsters came.

Eibon was more concerned with those that had made it through the main line of fire at the moment. There weren't more than perhaps two dozen of the creatures, but now they were using the docked craft inside the bay as cover as they worked their way forward, closing in on the position of the bay's defenders.

His rifle kicked in his hands as Eibon dropped one of the infected who had gotten through with a three-round burst that struck the creature's head like a sledgehammer coming down on an overripe melon. Black blood, bone fragments, and brain matter exploded in a rain of gore from the top of the infected's neck where its head had been a fraction of a second before.

"Sir!" one of the soldiers from the bridge yelled at Eibon.

It took Eibon a moment to realize who he was talking to. He wasn't used to being called sir.

"What is it?" Eibon yelled back.

"We've got movement behind us!" the soldier answered over the cacophony of gunfire and snarls.

Eibon sent another of the infected back to Hell with a shot that blew its brains out the backside of its skull and then turned glance towards the other side of the hangar. His eyes bugged at what he saw there.

A young woman with blazing yellow eyes, dressed in a ragged and blood-stained lieutenant uniform, stood across the hangar from them, a missile launcher braced against her shoulder.

"Holy…!" Eibon screamed. He had no time to warn the others as the woman fired the weapon.

Eibon hit the floor of the hangar hard nearly dislocating his shoulder in the process. The missile streaked through the air above him on its path towards its target. The shuttle Captain Hall had been powering up exploded in a flash of light and flame that shook the entire hangar.

"Captain!" Eibon wailed, but he knew that Hall was dead. All hope of escaping the *Magnum* died with him. The missile had reduced the shuttle to little more than burning wreckage.

The blast had knocked everyone else from their feet, and the barrage of fire that had been holding the waves of infected in check was gone. Shrapnel from the shuttle had taken its toll on the others as well. Grey's body lay not more than a few feet from Eibon. A large, jagged piece of debris protruded from his spine, and a puddle of red was forming around his corpse where it lay.

Grey wasn't the only one killed in the blast either. One of the soldiers from the bridge and two of the officers had died from the shrapnel the exploding shuttle had flung into them.

Eibon rolled to his feet. "Everybody left alive, *run!*"

He knew the order was pointless. There was nowhere to run to. Anywhere they fled to, sooner or later, the infected would find them. The *Magnum* was a large ship, but even so, it would only be a matter of time until the infected caught up with them no matter where they hid.

Eibon considered making a run for it himself but didn't. Instead, he charged across the bay at the infected woman who with a single hand still clutched the heavy missile that had killed Captain Hall. If he had to die, he at least wanted some vengeance before he did.

Behind him, gunfire continued to intermix with the snarls of the infected as the others tried to run for it like he ordered them to and fight their way out of the hangar. The chaos worked to his advantage, keeping the rest of the infected engaged behind him so he could focus his attention on the woman who had killed his friend.

He hadn't known Captain Hall well, but in the short time they'd fought together, Eibon had learned that the captain truly was a man worthy of his rank and a good man as well. He hadn't deserved to die like he had. No one on the *Magnum* had deserved what the infected had done to them. Now, it was time for the creatures to pay, and the woman was as good a place to start as any. Eibon could tell from how she held herself that there was something different about her. Unlike the other infected he had encountered, a keen intelligence flickered in her eyes.

The woman cocked her to the side and shot him a wide smile that showed the red-slicked rows of razor-like teeth inside her mouth. Was she laughing at him?

The big one came out of nowhere, plowing into him as he ran. The force of the impact lifted Eibon from the hangar floor and sent him flying. He landed hard again, this time with the sickening, cracking noise of breaking bone.

Eibon cried out in pain as the weight of his own body snapped his left arm near his elbow. The break was a bad one. He could see the white of bone poking through his flesh as blood streamed in rivers of red over the length of his arm as he got to his feet. Somehow, he had managed to keep his grip on his weapon and felt pride at that fact. He jerked its barrel up towards the hulking monster of an infected man that came roaring down on him. Squeezing the trigger, he kept it tight, emptying the rifle's magazine into the big man with blazing yellow eyes. The bullets gutted the big infected man. His guts spilled from the gaping holes they blew in his stomach. Purple, red-slicked tendrils flopped onto the floor. Still, the big man came on. Eibon ducked beneath the big man's outstretched grasping hands and ran, popping his spent magazine as he went. The big infected whirled around, jerking out the strands of intestines that dangled from him, and flinging them away. His face was a grimace of pain but anger blazed in his eyes. Eibon slammed a fresh magazine home as he stared at the big infected in horror. By all rights, the big man should be dead.

With a roar, the big man came at him again. Eibon raised his rifle and opened up on the big man again. Bullets ripped chunks of flesh from the big man's shoulders and chest. The damage they inflicted didn't even slow him down. It was as if there was some force driving on the big man's body that went beyond his own will. Eibon adjusted his aim, going for the big man's head too late. The barrel of his rifle came up just as the big man reached him. One of the big man's hands closed on Eibon's rifle. The pressure of the man's grip crunched the metal of the rifle, rendering it useless.

The infected woman who had killed Captain Hall was watching it all. Eibon saw that she had dropped her missile launcher at her feet. She appeared to be in some sort of trance-like state. Her body swayed back and forth, though her eyes remained locked on him and the big infected. Eibon put two and two together, making the irrational leap to the conclusion that the infected woman was the force driving the big man on, though he should he be dead.

There was no more time to think though as the big man's fist flew towards his head. Eibon ducked the blow as he yanked his sidearm from the holster on his hip. He came up, pressing the barrel of his pistol against the underside of the big man's chin and squeezed the trigger. His pistol bucked in his grasp as it spat a round that tore through the big man's head and exited the top of his skull. Finally, the big man fell. Eibon sidestepped his collapsing form as it thudded to the hangar floor.

Covered in sweat, his heart pounding against his ribs, Eibon looked at the infected woman. She had come out of her trance-like state. She was flinging her arms about in open rage as she shrieked a high-pitched wail that blew out the windows of the shuttles docked inside the hangar bay. The intensity of her cry was so great that it drove Eibon to his knees, hands clasped over his ears. His pistol clattered to the floor next to where he fell.

As the woman's cry stopped, she charged at him. Eibon saw blood from his ears on his hands as he snatched up his pistol. His ears were ringing so loudly that the hangar seemed to be spinning around him. His trembling hands brought up his pistol in a two-handed grip, aimed at the woman as she ran towards him. His first shot slashed a groove along the side length of her left cheek. His second struck her in the mouth as he continued to try to put a bullet in her brain. It blew out several of her teeth in a spray of black blood. His third shot missed the woman entirely. There wasn't time for a fourth.

The infected woman slapped his pistol from his hands. She grabbed him under his chin, holding his face tight, her claws sinking into his flesh. Eibon struggled against her hold, straining to break free as she raised his face upwards so that she could meet his eyes.

Eibon looked into the burning yellow orbs of her eyes and saw the very depths of Hell within them.

"I...am..." the woman began, but Eibon slipped the knife on the side of his boot from its sheath and sunk its blade deep into her throat. She released him, staggering backwards, as her hands moved to the hole his knife had left in her as he had jerked it free.

He could tell she was still trying to talk but all that was coming out her was a series of sickening gargling sounds.

Eibon didn't want to even think about what the fact that this infected woman remembered how to use a missile launcher and could talk. If she had relearned those things, what else would she remember given time?

The other infected in the hangar bay were watching their fight. Not a single one of them moved to come at him. Somehow, Eibon sensed that the woman's will was keeping them from doing so. She wanted him for herself.

Spotting a crate of weapons nearby, Eibon made a run for it. He reached it, flipping open the two mechanisms that held it closed. The crate contained a tri-barrel, a belt fed, heavy weapon. Eibon slipped the end of the ammo belt into the weapon's side before he lifted it out of the case. As he did so, he turned to see the woman coming at him again. His ears popped. The pain of them doing so almost blinded him, but suddenly he could hear again.

"Frag you, lady!" Eibon shouted as the barrels of the weapon whirred and spun. A stream of high-velocity rounds erupted from them to tear the woman to shreds as she approached him. They blew her arms and legs from her torso and sent her head bouncing across the floor of the hangar bay as her body was reduced black, blood-smeared chunks of flying meat.

With her death, the other infected sprang into action. The hangar echoed with their snarling cries of hunger and rage. Eibon hosed the front line of their ranks as they charged him, sending dozens of the creatures to Hell in a blaze of bullets. He kept firing as he backpedaled towards the open side door of the shuttle the crate he had taken the tri-barrel from looked to have been in position to be loaded onto.

As soon as he reached the shuttle's door, he tossed the tri-barrel away and dove through it. Eibon's fist slammed into the door's controls. It slid closed behind him. The infected chasing him smashed into like a tidal wave, shaking the shuttle.

Eibon's head wiped around to look towards the shuttle's forward window as he heard more infected slapping their hands against it. Others had leaped on top of the shuttle and were tearing at its armored hull with their claws. There was so many of them. Given time, he knew they would get into the shuttle with him one way or another.

The places where the female infected had dug her claws into the flesh of his chin burned. He could feel the virus inside of him trying to shut down his brain and take control. Ignoring the fire in his wounds and that pulsed through his veins, Eibon raced towards the shuttle's controls. Flinging himself into the pilot's seat, he glanced up at the infected raging against the shuttle's window. Already cracks were forming in it from their fury as they continued to pound on it and chip away at its reinforced glass with the almost supernatural strength of their claws.

Eibon wasn't a pilot, but he knew enough about shuttles to bring its power core online and set it to overload. Once he had done so, he slumped in the pilot's seat, watching the core's power level build up on the data screen of the console in front of him.

As the shuttle's power core reached critical mass, its forward window shattered. One of the infected came plunging towards him, its hands outstretched, grabbing for his face. In the instant before those hands closed on him, Eibon and the infected died in a blast of light and heat that blossomed outward from the exploding shuttle to consume the entirety of the hangar bay.

****

Captain Allen knew that Captain Hall and the survivors aboard the *Magnum* were planning on abandoning her. They were supposed to be bringing the parts needed to repair the *Pickman*'s primary drive with them. Over an hour had passed since the *Magnum*'s XO, Grey, had informed him for Hall's plan. He sat in his command chair, watching an image of the *Magnum* on the forward view screen.

"Sir!" his sensor tech yelled at him. "There's a power build up inside the *Magnum*'s hangar bay."

Before Captain Allen could even respond, he saw an explosion burst into space from the *Magnum*'s hangar. In its wake, secondary explosions detonated along the length of the ship as the *Magnum* broke apart.

There was silence on the *Pickman*'s bridge as Captain Allen and his crew watched all their hope die with the disintegrating battleship. Captain Allen didn't know how much time passed before one of his crewmen finally spoke up.

"Captain?" Hailey, his comm. officer, asked.

Captain Allen shook his head in an attempt to clear it.

"What do we do now, sir?" Barry, his acting XO, asked.

Captain Allen tried to pull himself together and stay professional, though it was all he could do to keep from weeping openly.

"The blink drive is dead?" Captain Allen asked.

"You know it is, sir," Barry cautiously reminded him.

"But the sensors remain functional?" Captain Allen turned to Barry.

"Yes, sir," Barry answered. "I have the results of the scan of this system you asked for."

"And are there any inhabitable planets within range of our sub-blink drive?"

"One, sir."

"Helm, set a course for it at the maximum speed we can muster without tearing this ship apart," Captain Allen ordered. The *Pickman* was so damaged that only her structural shields and the patches he and his crew had slapped into place were all that was holding her together.

"Yes, sir," his helmsman answered.

Captain Allen wanted to say something that would give the others on the bridge hope, something to lift their spirits, but the best he could managed was, "For better or worse, folks, it looks like we've found our new home. Let's hope it's a friendly place."

END

Eric S Brown is the author of numerous book series including the Bigfoot War series, the Kaiju Apocalypse series (with Jason Cordova), the Crypto-Squad series (with Jason Brannon), the Homeworld series (With Tony Faville and Jason Cordova), the Jack Bunny Bam series, and the A Pack of Wolves series. Some of his stand alone books include War of the Worlds plus Blood Guts and Zombies, World War of the Dead, Taskforce: The Bug Wars, Kraken, Alien Battalion, Sasquatch Lake, Kaiju Armageddon, Megalodon, Megalodons, and Megalodon Apocalypse to name only a few. His short fiction has been published hundreds of times in the small press in beyond including markets like the Onward Drake and Black Tide Rising anthologies from Baen Books, the Grantville Gazette, the SNAFU Military horror anthology series, and Walmart World magazine. He has done the novelizations for such films as Boggy Creek: The Legend is True (Studio 3 Entertainment) and The Bloody Rage of Bigfoot (Great Lake films). The first book of his Bigfoot War series was adapted into a feature film by Origin Releasing in 2014. Werewolf Massacre at Hell's Gate was the second his books to be adapted into film in 2015. In addition to his fiction, Eric also writes an award-winning comic book news column entitled "Comics in a Flash." Eric lives in North Carolina with his wife and two children where he continues to write tales of the hungry dead, blazing guns, and the things that lurk in the woods.

CHECK OUT OTHER GREAT
SCIENCE FICTION BOOKS

SALVAGE MERC ONE
by Jake Bible

Joseph Laribeau was born to be a Marine in the Galactic Fleet. He was born to fight the alien enemies known as the Skrang Alliance and travel the galaxy doing his duty as a Marine Sergeant. But when the War ended and Joe found himself medically discharged, the best job ever was over and he never thought he'd find his way again.

Then a beautiful alien walked into his life and offered him a chance at something even greater than the Fleet, a chance to serve with the Salvage Merc Corp.

Now known as Salvage Merc One Eighty-Four, Joe Laribeau is given the ultimate assignment by the SMC bosses. To his surprise it is neither a military nor a corporate salvage. Rather, Joe has to risk his life for one of his own. He has to find and bring back the legend that started the Corp.

SERENGETI
by J.B. Rockwell

It was supposed to be an easy job: find the Dark Star Revolution Starships, destroy them, and go home. But a booby-trapped vessel decimates the Meridian Alliance fleet, leaving Serengeti—a Valkyrie class warship with a sentient AI brain—on her own; wrecked and abandoned in an empty expanse of space. On the edge of total failure, Serengeti thinks only of her crew. She herds the survivors into a lifeboat, intending to sling them into space. But the escape pod sticks in her belly, locking the cryogenically frozen crew inside.

Then a scavenger ship arrives to pick Serengeti's bones clean. Her engines dead, her guns long silenced, Serengeti and her last two robots must find a way to fight the scavengers off and save the crew trapped inside her.

CHECK OUT OTHER GREAT SCIENCE FICTION BOOKS

IN PERPETUITY
by Jake Bible

For two thousand years, Earth and her many colonies across the galaxy have fought against the Estelian menace. Having faced overwhelming losses, the CSC has instituted the largest military draft ever, conscripting millions into the battle against the aliens. Major Bartram North has been tasked with the unenviable task of coordinating the military education of hundreds of thousands of recruits and turning them into troops ready to fight and die for the cause.

As Major North struggles to maintain a training pace that the CSC insists upon, he realizes something isn't right on the Perpetuity. But before he can investigate, the station dissolves into madness brought on by the physical booster known as pharma. Unfortunately for Major North, that is not the only nightmare he faces- an armada of Estelian warships is on the edge of the solar system and headed right for Earth!

BATTLEFIELD MARS
by David Robbins

Several centuries into the future, Earth has established three colonies on Mars. No indigenous life has been discovered, and humankind looks forward to making the Red Planet their own.

Then 'something' emerges out of a long-extinct volcano and doesn't like what the humans are doing.

Captain Archard Rahn, United Nations Interplanetary Corps, tries to stem the rising tide of slaughter. But the Martians are more than they seem, and it isn't long before Mars erupts in all-out war.

CHECK OUT OTHER GREAT SCIENCE FICTION BOOKS

FURNACE
by Joseph Williams

On a routine escort mission to a human colony, Lieutenant Michael Chalmers is pulled out of hyper-sleep a month early. The RSA Rockne Hummel is well off course and—as the ship's navigator—it's up to him to figure out why. It's supposed to be a simple fix, but when he attempts to identify their position in the known universe, nothing registers on his scans. The vessel has catapulted beyond the reach of starlight by at least a hundred trillion light-years. Then a planetary-mass object materializes behind them. It's burning brightly even without a star to heat it. Hundreds of damaged ships are locked in its orbit. The crew discovers there are no life-signs aboard any of them. As system failures sweep through the Hummel, neither Chalmers nor the pilot can prevent the vessel from crashing into the surface near a mysterious ancient city. And that's where the real nightmare begins.

LUNA
by Rick Chesler

On the threshold of opening the moon to tourist excursions, a private space firm owned by a visionary billionaire takes a team of non-astronauts to the lunar surface. To address concerns that the moon's barren rock may not hold long-term allure for an uber-wealthy clientele, the company's charismatic owner reveals to the group the ultimate discovery: life on the moon.

But what is initially a triumphant and world-changing moment soon gives way to unrelenting terror as the team experiences firsthand that despite their technological prowess, the moon still holds many secrets.

www.ingramcontent.com/pod-product-compliance
Lightning Source LLC
Chambersburg PA
CBHW022026170626
46808CB00003B/1077